William M. Graydon

In the Days of Washington

A Story of the American Revolution

William M. Graydon

In the Days of Washington
A Story of the American Revolution

ISBN/EAN: 9783337227227

Printed in Europe, USA, Canada, Australia, Japan

Cover: Foto ©Andreas Hilbeck / pixelio.de

More available books at **www.hansebooks.com**

IN THE

DAYS OF WASHINGTON

A STORY OF THE AMERICAN REVOLUTION

———

BY

WILLIAM ·MURRAY GRAYDON

THE PENN PUBLISHING COMPANY

PHILADELPHIA MDCCCXCVI

CONTENTS

IN THE DAYS OF WASHINGTON

CHAPTER I

IN WHICH MR. NOAH WAXPENNY INTRODUCES HIMSELF

IT was an evening in the first week in February, 1778. Supper was over in the house of Cornelius De Vries, which stood on Green Street, Philadelphia, and in that part of the town known as the Northern Liberties. Agatha De Vries, the elderly and maiden sister of Cornelius, had washed and put away the dishes and had gone around the corner to gossip with a neighbor.

The light shed from two copper candlesticks and from the fire made the sitting-room look very snug and cozy. In one corner stood a tall clock-case, flanked by a white pine settee and a chest of drawers. A spider legged writing-desk stood near the tile lined fireplace, over which was a row of china dishes—very rare at that time. The floor was white and sanded, and the walls were hung with a few paintings and colored prints.

Cornelius De Vries, a well-to-do and retired merchant, occupied a broad-armed chair at one side of the table that stood in the middle of the room. He was a very stately old gentleman of sixty, with a clean-shaven and wrinkled face. He wore a wig, black stockings, a coat and vest of broadcloth, and low shoes with silver buckles. His features betrayed his Dutch origin, as did also the long-stemmed pipe he was smoking, and the glass of Holland schnapps at his elbow.

At the opposite side of the table sat Nathan Stanbury, a handsome lad, neatly dressed in gray homespun and starched linen, and of a size and strength that belied his seventeen years. His cheeks were ruddy with health, and his curly chestnut hair matched the deep brown of his eyes.

Nathan was a student at the College of Philadelphia, and the open book in his hand was a Latin Horace. But he found it difficult to fix his mind on the lesson, and his thoughts were constantly straying far from the printed pages. Doubtless the wits of Cornelius De Vries were wool-gathering in the same direction, for he had put aside the hated evening paper, " The Royal Gazette," and was dreamily watching the blue curls of smoke as they puffed upward from his pipe. Now he would frown severely, and now his eyes would twinkle and his cheeks distend in a grim sort of smile.

There was much for the loyal people of the town to talk and think about at that time. For nearly six months the British army, under General Howe, had occupied Philadelphia in ease and comfort, while at Valley Forge Washington's ragged soldiers were starving and freezing in the wintry weather, their heroic commander bearing in dignified silence the censure and complaint that were freely vented by his countrymen. Black and desperate, indeed, seemed the cause of the United American Colonies in that winter of 1777–78, and as yet no light of cheer was breaking on the horizon.

After grappling for the twentieth time with his lesson, Nathan suddenly closed the book and tossed it on the table.

"I can't translate Latin to-night, Master De Vries," he exclaimed. "It's no use trying. I wish I was down-town. Perhaps a walk in the fresh air will compose my mind."

The merchant answered only by a negative shake of the head, as he filled and ignited his pipe for the third time.

"Yes, you are right," Nathan said, resignedly. "I suppose I should keep indoors as much as possible to avoid suspicion, and I may be needed again shortly—"

Rat, tat, tat! Low and clear rang a knocking on the panels of the front door.

"There!" exclaimed Nathan, jumping up and running into the hall. The opening of the door revealed a short man standing on the lower step; it was too dark to see his face plainly.

Without a word he handed the lad a slip of paper, and then strode swiftly off down the street.

Nathan closed and locked the door, and hurried to the light of the candles. He unfolded the paper and read aloud the following brief message, written in a small and legible hand:

"Come to the Indian Queen at once. Thee will find friends waiting thy trusty services."

The lad's eyes sparkled, and his cheeks were flushed with excitement. "Another ride to Valley Forge," he said, eagerly. "How glad my father will be to see me! And it is a night ride this time, Master De Vries. I'll warrant 'tis a matter of great importance."

"Not so loud, lad," cautioned the merchant. "But how comes it the word was trusted to paper? Did you know the messenger?"

"It was Pulling, the deaf and dumb hostler from the tavern," Nathan replied. "Doubtless they have just heard news, and could not spare time to seek the usual messenger. Pulling is trustworthy enough and, of course, since he can't speak—"

"It was imprudent to write," interrupted the merchant, "but I dare say they could do no better. Certainly, the summons is urgent, since it calls thee out at night."

"Yes, I must go at once," said Nathan, "and without so much as a change of clothes. If the service is what I think it to be I will hardly be back by morning." As he spoke, he abstractedly dropped the slip of paper into the side pocket of his jacket, and moved toward the hall.

"May the good God bring you back in safety," Cornelius De Vries said, earnestly. "I love you dearly, lad, even as I love your father, and I would not see you come to harm. I have long mistrusted these perilous doings, and yet for the sake of the cause—"

"To save my oppressed country I would risk life ten times over," declared Nathan. "If there were no work for me to do here I should be fighting with our brave soldiers. But there is really no danger, Master De Vries. You know how often I have been back and forth."

"But not at night, lad."

"So much the better, with the darkness to shelter me," replied Nathan. "I must be off now. Good-bye, and don't worry."

He put on his cap and briefly returned the pressure of the old man's hand. A moment later the door had closed behind him and he was walking rapidly down the silent street. The weather had changed a day or two before, and there was a suggestiveness of spring in the mild, damp air.

Richard Stanbury, the father of Nathan, had come from England to America in 1760, at the age of twenty-six. He brought a wife with him—a pretty and refined woman—and they settled in Philadelphia. The next year Nathan was born, and five years later his mother died. The blow was a severe one to Richard Stanbury, and, the Quaker City being now distasteful to him, he removed with his son to New England. He accompanied the Connecticut colony to the Wyoming Valley in Pennsylvania —which grant they had purchased from the

Delaware Indians—and took part in the long struggle with the Pennsylvania settlers who were found in unjust possession. When the warfare finally came to a peaceful end he settled down to a life of farming and hunting in that earthly paradise.

Richard Stanbury was a handsome and refined man, and a highly educated one. All with whom he came in contact were quick to realize his superiority, but in spite of that and his reserved nature, he made friends readily. He closely guarded the secret of his past, whatever it was, not even opening the pages to his son. But at times he hinted mysteriously at a great change that was likely to happen in the future, and he took pains to teach Nathan reading, writing, and history, and the rules of gentlemanly conduct. There was deep affection between father and son, and that the lad did not seek to know the mystery of the past was because he respected his parent's silence. He grew up to be brave and strong, generous and fearless, and few companions of his age could shoot with such skill or track game so untiringly through the forest.

Soon after the great struggle for liberty began, and the colonies were in arms to throw off the British yoke, many of the settlers of Wyoming left their families and the old men at home and marched away to join Washington. Richard Stanbury went with them; he was Captain Stanbury now, and commanded a company. Nathan, young as he was, burned to enlist and fight. But his father would not hear of this. He had long ago formed other plans for the lad, and now the time for them was ripe. To Philadelphia went Nathan, to attend the admirable college that the Quaker town boasted, and to find a happy home with Cornelius De Vries. The expense was to come out of the worthy merchant's pocket. He had claimed this right because of the long friendship between himself and Richard Stanbury, which dated from the latter's arrival in America.

So Nathan studied hard, a favorite with masters and pupils, while the first two years of the

Revolution scored their triumphs and adverses. But he was not content to let others do the fighting, and when the British occupied Philadelphia, in the fall of 1777, the lad found at last a chance to help the cause of freedom. Several loyal citizens of the town had secret means of getting information about the plans of the British officers. These men were friends of Cornelius De Vries, and they came to know that his young lodger was a plucky and intelligent lad, and one to be relied upon. So Nathan was frequently chosen to carry messages to the camp at Valley Forge, where he sometimes saw his father, and where he made the acquaintance of General Washington and other officers. It was a very simple plan, and one that was not likely to be suspected. The citizens were permitted to take their grain through the British lines to the grist-mill at Frankford, and the lad would ride out after dinner on this errand. While the grain was being ground it was an easy matter for him to gallop to and from the American camp, then returning to the city by night with his sacks of meal.

As Nathan hurried away from the Dutch merchant's house on this February evening, he knew that he was wanted for some service of more than ordinary importance. "This is the first time I have been sent for at night," he reflected, "and I guess it means a dash through the lines. The sentries don't allow any trips to mill after dark."

He looked up to find himself passing the British barracks, which fronted on Green Street from Second to Third, and had been built soon after Braddock's defeat. Howe's army now occupied them, and the red-coated sentry at the gate glanced sourly at the lad in the gloom. Nathan went on, carelessly whistling a snatch of a tune, and presently turned down Fourth Street. A few yards from the corner, where a narrow bar of light streamed across the pavement from an open window, he collided with some one coming from the opposite way; both came to a halt.

"Why don't you watch where you're going?" brusquely demanded the stranger, who looked to be about Nathan's age, and wore a new and well-fitting British uniform.

"I might ask you the same," Nathan responded pleasantly, "but I won't. You see it's so dark hereabouts, and—why, Godfrey! I didn't know you."

"Nathan Stanbury!" cried the other, in keenest surprise and pleasure. "How glad I am to see you!" He held out his hand expecting it to be taken.

"No; I can't," Nathan said gravely. "I— I'm sorry to see you in those clothes."

"And I'm proud of them. So you're as much of a patriot as ever? I thought you would turn."

"I'll never turn," declared Nathan. "I'm more of a patriot than I was, and some day I'll be a soldier—"

"Hush! don't air your opinions so loudly around here," cautioned Godfrey, in a good-natured tone. "I'm not going to quarrel with you, Nathan. Two such old friends as we are can surely meet without talking about the war. I can't forget that you saved my life once, and I will always be grateful."

"That sounds well from a Tory," interrupted Nathan. "Why don't you begin by being grateful to your country?"

The other flushed, and for a few embarrassing seconds nothing was said. Standing together in the stream of yellow lamp-light, the two lads looked strangely alike, a resemblance that others had frequently observed. They were of the same build and height, and had the same general features. Godfrey Spencer was older by a year, with black eyes and hair. Nathan's eyes and hair were deep brown.

"You are still attending college?" Godfrey finally said.

Nathan nodded. "When did you come back to town?" he asked.

"Two days ago," Godfrey replied, "with dispatches for General Clinton. You know I went with my mother to Long Island, and there

2

I enlisted in a—a Tory regiment. I was promoted to lieutenant a month ago, and now Major Langdon, who is stationed here, has promised me a place on his staff." The last words were spoken with evident pride.

"I'm sorry for you," said Nathan. "I can't wish you success, Godfrey, but I truly hope, for the sake of old times, that you won't get shot. I must go now. Good-bye."

Disregarding the other's appeal to return, Nathan walked rapidly down the street, ignorant of the fact—as was Godfrey—that a British officer had been watching both lads closely from the open and lighted window of the house in front of which they were standing.

"Who was that lad, Spencer?" he demanded.

"An old college friend, Major Langdon," replied Godfrey, a little startled by the question. "His people are rebels. I was trying to convert him."

"I mean his name, stupid, quick!"

"Nathan Stanbury," said Godfrey.

The major's face turned white, and something like an oath escaped his lips. His hands shook as they rested on the window-sill.

"I might have known," he muttered to himself. Then aloud: "Yonder is a bit of paper the lad dropped when he pulled out his handkerchief. Fetch it, Spencer."

Godfrey reluctantly picked up the paper, and Major Langdon opened the door to admit him.

A few months before Richard Stanbury's arrival in the Colonies there came from England to Philadelphia a merchant of London, Matthew Marsham by name. He was accompanied by his daughter, Betty Spencer, and her infant son Godfrey. Mrs. Spencer wore mourning for her husband, who had died recently. The merchant engaged in business, and prospered sufficiently to keep his little family in comfort and give his grandson a thorough education.

To college went Godfrey in due course, and here he and Nathan were classmates for nearly a year after the beginning of the Revolution, during which period they formed a warm boyish friendship.

On one occasion, while swimming in the Delaware, Nathan risked his own life to save Godfrey from drowning. But the growing animosities of the war finally began to draw the lads apart, for Godfrey's mother and grandfather were Tories. In the spring of 1777 Matthew Marsham died, and Mrs. Spencer removed with her son to Long Island, where she had friends living.

It was of this past friendship—so strongly recalled to-night—more than of his errand, that Nathan was thinking sadly as he kept on his way down-town. Frequently he crossed the street to avoid a group of drunken and riotous soldiers, or put on a careless gait and attitude as some mounted officer spurred barrackwards past him. He met but few others, for reputable citizens kept indoors after dark.

The Indian Queen tavern, one of the oldest and best known hostelries of the town, stood on South Fourth Street near Chestnut. The tap-room was empty when Nathan entered, and the secretly loyal landlord, Israel Jenkins, was taking his ease on a bench.

"Well, here I am," said Nathan. "Company in the back room again, eh?"

"Not this time, lad," replied Jenkins, with a wink of the eye. "The back room is too open for to-night's work. You'll find them—"

Sudden footsteps outside caused the landlord to bite off the sentence abruptly. "Get yourself yonder," he added, "and wait till I come. Quick! you mustn't be seen."

He pushed Nathan into a dark hall on one side of the room, leaving the door open several inches, and from his place of concealment the lad saw the new arrival enter the tavern.

He was a man who would have attracted attention in any surroundings, and was as likely to excite mirth as respect. His age was about fifty, and his tall, gaunt figure was dressed in rusty broadcloth, black stockings without knee or shoe buckles, and a gray cocked hat. He wore a flaxen wig, and a steel watch chain with seals dangled from his waistcoat. His face was smooth and of a parchment color, his nose abnormally large, and his eyes small and piggish. He had long white fingers, and he snapped them nervously as he nodded with an air of condescension to the landlord.

"Good evening, sir," he said, in an oily voice. "I would have a pot of your best brew, and an ounce of mild tobacco."

"I don't sell the last named," curtly replied Jenkins, who was by no means favorably impressed with his customer.

"But you will let me have a little, eh, my good friend? Here is some," tapping his breast pocket, "but the sea air has quite destroyed its flavor."

"You have lately crossed then?" asked Jenkins, who was always on the alert for news, and scented a present opportunity.

"But this day I arrived from England on the packet-boat 'Bristol,'" replied the stranger, "and right glad was I to put foot on solid ground. Thank you, my friend," he added, as Jenkins placed before him a tankard of ale and a twist of tobacco. "And now may I make bold to ask a little information of you?"

"Depends on what it is," growled Jenkins, his suspicions suddenly awakened.

"It is nothing harmful, sir; quite the contrary. Does not my face inspire confidence? Then you shall have my name. It is Noah Waxpenny, and I have the honor to be confidential clerk to the firm of Sharswood & Feeman, solicitors, Lincoln Inn, London."

"It's no odds if you were the king himself," imprudently replied Jenkins.

"Ha, very clever! A neat joke," laughed Mr. Waxpenny. "God save King George, and all his loyal subjects!"

"Amen to that!" muttered the landlord, aloud. "And God forgive the lie," he added to himself.

Mr. Noah Waxpenny chuckled, and half emptied the pewter at a draught. Then he leaned toward Jenkins in a confidential manner, and his next words were of so startling a nature that Nathan very nearly toppled against the door that separated him from the tap-room.

CHAPTER II

"I wish to learn the present whereabouts of
Richard Stanbury," said Mr. Waxpenny, slowly
and deliberately. "Under that name he came
from England to America in 1760, and a year
later he was known to be residing in Philadelphia with a wife and infant son. Can you give
me any information about him?"

With a heightened color Jenkins stared first
at the ceiling, and then shot a glance of apprehension at the hall door. "Stanbury ain't a
common name," he replied, by way of gaining
time, "but it seems like I've heard it some-
wheres or other. It might'n be Stanwix, now?"

"No, Stanbury—Richard Stanbury."

The landlord propped his elbows on the
counter and looked meditatively into vacancy.
"I've heard of Bow Street runners," he said to

himself, "and I misdoubt but this chap is one of the snaky varmints in disguise. It ain't likely Dick Stanbury is wanted over in England, but there's no telling. What am I going to do about it? I'll bet a ha'penny the lad's listening out yonder with both ears. I'll just lie low till I get my bearings—that's the safest plan."

During the course of this mental soliloquy he was cocking his head this way and that, and now he shook it in a manner that indicated profound and hopeless ignorance.

"If a golden guinea would jog your memory, why, here it is," suggested Mr. Waxpenny, displaying the coin.

"The gold wouldn't come amiss," said Jenkins, with a sigh, "but it ain't possible for me to earn it."

The law clerk pocketed the guinea. "It's unlikely that Richard Stanbury was in your walk of life, my man," said he, with quiet scorn. "Your ignorance is excusable."

"My what?"

"Your disability to remember," corrected

Mr. Waxpenny. "And now we'll try again. Can you tell me if Major Gerald Langdon, of the British cavalry, is stationed in this town ?"

"I seen by the 'Royal Gazette,' a fortnight ago, that he was in New York," replied Jenkins, truthfully enough. "What on earth is the game ?" he asked himself in amazement.

Mr. Waxpenny nodded his satisfaction. "There is one more person I wish to inquire about," he said. "Did you ever hear of—"

The rest of the sentence was drowned in a burst of noisy voices and shuffling feet, as half a dozen tipsy soldiers and marines swung round the corner and entered the tavern. The London law clerk looked disdainfully at the company, and then made a hasty exit. Having served his customers Jenkins left them with brimming mugs in hand, and darted into the hall, slamming the door behind him.

"Where are you, lad ?" he whispered.

"Here!" Nathan answered, hoarsely, from the darkness. "I have heard all, Mr. Jenkins.

What can it mean? Why did that man inquire for my father?"

"I haven't an idea," replied the landlord. "If he comes back I'll try to pump him. Meanwhile, it won't be amiss to tell your father there's a London chap seeking him."

"I'll do that," muttered Nathan. "But it's queer—"

"Don't bother about it," whispered Jenkins. "They're waiting for you up above—in the little room on the right at the head of the stairs. You'll see a light under the door. I must be off."

The landlord returned to his customers, and Nathan slowly ascended the stairs, still puzzling over the strange inquiries of Mr. Waxpenny. Guided by the glimmer of light, he entered a small bed-chamber—the identical room, in fact, in which Jefferson had written the Declaration of Independence two years before. Here the lad found Anthony Benezet and Timothy Matlack, two elderly and highly respectable Quaker citizens. A candle, standing on a small table between them, dimly revealed their solemn faces and sober, gray garments.

"Thee is late to-night," said Timothy Matlack.

"I was detained at several places," explained Nathan. "I came as quickly as I could."

"And is thee ready to serve us as before?"

"Ready and willing, sir."

"This is a task of greater peril and difficulty," said Anthony Benezet. "We have tidings for General Washington which cannot be conveyed verbally, and should reach him before morning. Here is the packet," drawing a sealed and folded paper from his bosom. "Thee must slip unseen through the enemy's lines. It is the only way."

"I will do it," Nathan replied firmly. "There are many weak places, and the night is dark. I am not afraid."

"Thou art a brave lad," said Anthony Benezet, "and God will protect thee. So, now hasten on thy journey. When thou hast passed the sentries, go to the house of Abel Sansom, on the

Germantown Road.   He will give thee a horse
for the ride to Valley Forge."

Nathan concealed the precious packet about
his clothes, and turned toward the door.

"Wait," said Timothy Matlack.   "Did thee
destroy the message I sent thee by Jenkins'
man?"

"I—I think I put it in my pocket," faltered
Nathan, making a hasty search.   "But it is not
here now, sir.   I fear I have lost it."

"Where, lad? not on the street?"

"Yes," Nathan admitted huskily, "up near
the barracks."   He remembered pulling out his
handkerchief while talking to Godfrey.   The
note must have fallen out then, and he shivered
to think of the possible consequences of the loss.

"What rashness and folly!" groaned Timothy Matlack.   "We are ruined, Anthony—"

"Do not blame the lad," said his companion.
"It was but a pardonable want of caution.   All
may be well if we can get safely out of the
house.   Go, Nathan—"

Too late!   Just then came a clatter of feet

from down-stairs, and a couple of sharp words of command, a confused tumult arose and Jenkins was heard expostulating in loud and indignant tones in the tap-room. Next a door banged open, and the lower hall echoed to the tread of booted feet.

For a few seconds after the disturbance began the occupants of the little room stared at one another in dazed terror.

"The note has been found," gasped Timothy Matlack, "and British soldiers have come to search the house. We will all be hanged!"

"They must catch us first," exclaimed Nathan, extinguishing the candle with a puff, and darting to the window. "We are trapped," he added, with a gloomy glance at the street below. "Two grenadiers are on the pavement."

"Thee may get out by the rear of the house," hoarsely replied Anthony Benezet. "Those papers will be our death-warrant if the enemy take them. Thee must escape, lad—thee must. Quick! there is not an instant to lose."

"But you?" demurred Nathan.

"Friend Matlack and myself will remain quietly here," replied the old Quaker. "The note can but cause suspicion. There will be no proof against us, with thee out of the way. Here, take this. I had forgotten to give it to thee. Use it only in self-defense." In the darkness he pressed a heavy, brass-barreled pistol into the lad's hands.

"I will do my best," muttered Nathan. "If I am shot tell my father—" A lump rose in his throat, and without finishing the sentence he opened the door and stepped into the hall. Fortunately the invading party had halted below while Jenkins tardily fetched them a light, and now they were but two-thirds the distance up the staircase. In the front was a stern and handsome officer, with a naked sword in one hand and a glass lantern held high in the other. The flashing light shone behind him on the red coats and fierce countenances of half a dozen grenadiers.

Nathan saw all this at a brief glance, and recognized, with a thrill of anger, the face of

Godfrey Spencer among his foes.   He was himself instantly discovered as he turned and sped
along the hall.

"Halt, in the King's name!" roared the officer.   "Halt or die!"

On dashed Nathan, his heart thumping with
terror as the din and clatter of pursuit rang behind him.   He knew all about the house and
its surroundings, and a dozen strides brought
him to an angle of the hall.   He slipped round
the corner, and dimly saw, twenty feet ahead, a
small window that opened from the rear of the
house.

He was but half way to it when a bright light
streamed over him, and glancing backward he
saw the officer turn the angle at the head of his
men. Eager shouts told that they believed their
victim to be trapped.

It was a terrible crisis for the lad.   Either
he must check the enemy or abandon hope of
escape, and he realized this in the flash of a
second.   He halted, faced about, and took quick
aim with his pistol.

“Look out, Major Langdon,” cried a warning voice. “He’s going to shoot.”

Bang! The thunderous report shook the building. The shattered lantern crashed to the floor, followed by total darkness, a yell of pain, and a volley of curses and threats.

Amid the drifting smoke Nathan darted on to the window, threw up the sash, and let it fall with a clatter as he vaulted safely down upon the low roof of a shed.

He was just in time. Crack! crack! crack! —bullets whistled overhead, and broken glass and splinters showered about him as he half tumbled, half climbed to the ground. In a trice he was through the stable-yard and over a wall into Third Street, across that deserted thoroughfare, and speeding through a dark and narrow lane in the direction of the Delaware River.

There was dull shouting and outcry behind Nathan as he ran on, still clutching the empty pistol, and keeping a keen watch right and left; but he heard no close pursuit, and there were

3

no dwelling-houses on the lane to imperil his present safety.

"I'm going the wrong way," he said to himself, "but I daren't turn now. I hope I didn't kill that British officer—I never shot at any one before, and I hated to do it. One of the soldiers called him Major Langdon—why, that's the man who is going to put Godfrey on his staff, and the same that the London law clerk was inquiring about. Well, if I killed him I'm not to blame. It was in self-defense, and for my country's sake. If I'm caught they'll surely hang me—but I'm not going to be caught. These dispatches," feeling to make sure he had the precious packet, "must be saved from the enemy, and it won't be my fault if I don't deliver them at Valley Forge before morning."

The plucky lad had now reached Second Street, and finding no one in sight, he turned up-town on a rapid walk. He had passed Market Street and was near Arch when he heard faint shouts, and looking back he saw a group of dark figures in pursuit.

" They've tracked me clear from the tavern," he muttered, " and it won't be easy to give them the slip."

He began to run now, with the hue and cry swelling behind him. He did not dare to turn into Arch Street, seeing people moving here and there in both directions; so he continued up Second, slinking along in the shadow of the houses.

From a doorstep across the way some one shouted, and the human blood-hounds down the street caught up the cry with hoarse energy. The rush of many feet rang on the night air, and the tumult was rapidly spreading to the more remote quarters of the town.

Nathan ran doggedly and swiftly on, looking in vain for a place of hiding, and knowing that the occasional lamp-posts he passed revealed his flying form to the enemy. Above Race Street a sour-visaged man—evidently a Tory citizen— leapt forward from one side with a demand to stop. " Get out of the way," the lad muttered fiercely, aiming his empty weapon. The coward fell back with lusty shouting, which was heard and understood by the approaching soldiers.

Breathless and panting, Nathan turned west into Vine Street. With flagging strength and courage he kept on in his flight, realizing that unless some unforeseen help intervened he must soon be caught. Louder and nearer rang the roar of the pursuit, and a glance behind showed him the eager mob, led by red-coated grenadiers, within a hundred yards.

With a desperate spurt the lad pushed on. Up the street beyond him he heard cries and saw people running excitedly. "It's no use; I'm trapped," he muttered, and just then he made a discovery that sent a thrill of hope to his heart.

On Vine Street, a few yards from Cable Lane, was the house of Mr. Whitehead. Here Colonel Abercrombie was quartered, and a horse belonging to that officer, or to a visitor of rank, was standing before the door in care of a small boy. It was a large and handsome bay, and from each saddle-bag peeped the shiny butt of a pistol.

"What's the fuss about?" asked the small boy—who was Mr. Whitehead's son Jonas—as the fugitive pulled up breathlessly in front of him. "All that mob ain't chasing you, are they? Did you steal something?"

"No, but I'm going to," panted Nathan, with make-believe ferocity. He lifted the empty pistol. "Give me that horse. Don't make a whimper. I'll shoot you."

Terrified by the threat and weapon, Jonas let go the bridle and fled to the pavement. Nathan swung himself into the saddle, clapped feet in the stirrups, and gave the bridle a tug that swung the horse around and started it across the street. The rush and roar of the pursuers rang in his ears, blending with a shrill cry from Jonas. He heard the house door fly open, and the voices of Colonel Abercrombie and other officers raised in a profane howl. Then he was clattering madly up the dark roadway of Cable Lane, with the din and tumult ebbing fainter and fainter behind him.

On his stolen steed the lad cleared street after street at a gallop, making turns here and there, but trending mainly in the direction he wanted to go. Men and women in night-caps flung shutters open to look out, and called to people in the street as he whirled by. He had thrown his empty pistol away, and had taken from the holster a fresh one, which he held ready for use in his left hand.

Soon vacant lots began to take the place of houses, and lighted windows and startled citizens were seen less frequently. Nathan ventured to check his horse and listen. Far behind he heard the dull pounding of hoofs, telling him that some of his pursuers had found mounts and were on the track again. With a glance around to get his bearings he pushed on at a rapid trot to the open country, thinking this gait more proper for the half-formed plan he had against the coming and unavoidable emergency. He knew the locality, but not so well as he could have desired.

"The lines are some place about here," he muttered half aloud, "what shall I do? Trust to a dash to take me through, or abandon the horse and try it on foot? I must decide before the pickets—"

"Halt! who comes?" The gruff command rang out from ten feet ahead, where a shadowy form had suddenly risen from the darkness of the open field.

"Friend!" called Nathan, and with that he drove the stirrups so hard that his horse bounded forward on a gallop—straight for the dumfounded sentinel. There was a futile shot in air, a yell of pain, and then the Britisher was down under the cruel hoofs.

Nathan and his galloping steed swept on, while behind them the night blazed with red flashes, and echoed to musket shots, oaths, and scurrying feet.

"Safe at last!" the lad cried exultantly, and even as he spoke a jangle of equipments and a patter of hoofs on the turf gave the lie to his words. He had stumbled not on one or two pickets, but on a dismounted patroling party watching for deserters, who had been stepping

off rather frequently of late through this weak
part of the lines — mostly Hessians who had
taken a fancy to the country.

Nathan did not lose heart, black as his
chances seemed. He urged his horse to its top
speed, and the noble animal did gallantly. For
five minutes the chase thundered on, the enemy
slowly but surely gaining. A glance showed
the lad that his pursuers were less than two
hundred yards behind, and when he looked forward again it was to see the river Schuylkill
looming dark and quiet under the canopy of
stars.

No time to hesitate. Over and down the bluff
plunged horse and rider, their disappearance
being the signal for a rain of bullets. Splash!
splash! they were in the water now, and the
gallant steed was breasting waves and current
and slush ice as he swam toward the opposite
bank and safety, with the lad out of the saddle
and clinging to the flowing mane.

Now they were at mid-stream—the river was
narrower—and from the rear bank the halted

dragoons opened fire. Crack, crack, crack!— the balls whistled and sputtered harmlessly. It was too dark for good aim, and there was little in sight to aim at.

But keen eyes spied a boat moored in the bushes, and two soldiers were quickly in it and paddling after the fugitive. They were gaining rapidly, as Nathan saw by turning his head. Clinging to the horse's mane with one hand he snapped the pistol that he still held in the other. It was wet, and would not go off. He snatched the second from the unsubmerged saddle-bag, aimed and fired. With the report, the soldier who was paddling tossed up his arms and fell back with a hoarse cry. His comrade rose to his feet in the swaying boat, now but six yards away, and leveled his musket with a terrible oath.

Flash! bang! the gallant horse quivered, whinnied with pain, and swung helplessly around with the current. Nathan's hand let go the bridle, and the black waters closed over the lad's head.

CHAPTER III

IN WHICH NATHAN BECOMES A SOLDIER

NATHAN's sudden disappearance indicated that the bullet had struck him also, but such was not the case. He knew the horse was shot the instant the report rang out, and his object in bobbing under was twofold; to escape the animal's struggles and to deceive the soldier. Letting himself sink a few feet, he dived still deeper, and then swam beneath the surface toward shore. In spite of his clothes he covered a good distance, and when lack of breath forced him to the top he was within ten yards of the bank.

The watchful and suspecting dragoon spied the lad at once, and announced his discovery to the rest of the party by a shout, as he picked up the paddle and drove the boat nearer. On coming within the same range as before he snatched the musket from his dead or dying comrade, and again drew a bead on his intended victim.

Just at this point, when he was nearly to the shore, Nathan looked back and saw his danger. He was all but exhausted, and he knew that he had not a ghost of a chance to escape. He was too weak even to dive, and for a terrible second or two, while his enemy made sure of his aim, he expected instant death as he struggled feebly on.

But an undreamed of deliverance was at hand. From the near-by edge of the bank, in front of the lad, came a flash and a report. He glanced in bewilderment over his shoulder in time to see the murderous dragoon drop his unfired weapon and pitch head first into the water. The body sank at once, and the boat drifted on in pursuit of the dead horse.

Nathan swam to shore, scarcely able to credit his good fortune, and no sooner had he planted his trembling feet on the bank than a stalwart figure rose before him out of the gloom—a Hessian with bristling mustache, a blue and yellow uniform, and a brass plate on his tall, black cap.

He uttered a few angry words in German as he stared at the lad.

"You saved my life," said Nathan, who was quick to see how the land lay, "and I thank you for it."

"Och, I mean not to," the Hessian replied, in broken English. "I think you vas a comrade whom I watch for. You are American, eh? And you escape from the British?"

"Yes," boldly admitted Nathan.

The Hessian hesitated a moment. "You come mit me," he said. "This no safe place to stay."

Nathan was of the same mind, and he followed his companion up the bank and then into the woods, while the angry voices of the British dragoons grew faint in the rear. As they went along the Hessian explained that he had deserted that evening, and was to have been joined by another man from his company. He had taken Nathan to be that expected comrade. "I will look for Hans no longer," he added. "He may be dead or captured."

"Why did you run away?" asked Nathan, who had a thorough contempt for a deserter.

The Hessian was not angered by the question.

"Vy should I not?" he replied. "I haf no quarrel mit the colonists, and I like not to fight mit King Shorge for hire. In my native Anspach I get leedle pay und poor foot. I like America, and I alretty spike the language. Ach, is it not so?"

"Yes, you'll do," assented Nathan.

"I spike it better soon," the Hessian added. "And now vere you go?"

"To the American lines," Nathan answered. "I'll take you there if you wish."

"Nein, nein," the man replied; shaking his head vigorously. "Your general vill make me fight, und I haf enough of it. You go your vay und I go mit mine."

He was plainly unwilling to disclose his plans, and the lad did not care to press him. So, with a hearty hand-shake, they separated, the deserter striding off toward the west, while Nathan turned northward.

To reach the Germantown Road from the lad's present location would have meant a re-crossing of the Schuylkill and a long detour out of his nearest course—a plan not to be contemplated for a moment. After parting from the Hessian he squeezed the water out of his clothes, dried the dispatches as much as he could, and then tramped for half an hour through the dark woods and open fields. Coming to a road that he recognized, he pushed on more rapidly, and was soon knocking at the door of a loyal farmhouse. Down came the proprietor, nightcap on head and gun in hand, and on learning what was wanted he willingly loaned the lad his old mare and a pistol, on condition that both should be returned within a day or two.

Nathan mounted in haste and rode off. Mile after mile slipped from under the flying hoofs and no enemy barred the way. As dawn was breaking a gruff voice challenged him, and he knew he had reached the outer picket lines at Valley Forge.

The lad was known by name and reputation,

and after a short wait he was taken in charge by an officer and conducted through the camp. There was much of interest to be seen. The narrow streets were waking up to the day's activity, and ragged and starved-looking men were issuing from the little huts. Some were building fires and others carrying wood. Night pickets, just released from duty, were stumbling sleepily toward their quarters. Wan and hollow faces peeped from the windows of the hospitals, and here and there a one-legged soldier hobbled along on crutches.

Nathan and the officer presently reached the angle formed by the junction of the Schuylkill River and Valley Creek, where stood the large stone house that served for headquarters. The sentries passed them through the yard, and thence into the dining-room of the house. Here, early as was the hour, the American commander sat at breakfast. With him were two of his officers—Baron Steuben and General Knox.

"A messenger for you, General," said the lad's companion, Lieutenant Wills. "He left

Philadelphia last night and had the hardest kind of a time to get through. I thought you had better see him at once."

With this the lieutenant left the room, and Washington drew his chair a little out from the table. His grave and somewhat haggard face lit up with a smile of welcome as he looked at Nathan.

"So you are here again, Master Stanbury," he said, "and what do you bring me this time?"

"Dispatches from Anthony Benezet, sir," replied Nathan, drawing the precious packet from his bosom.

Washington opened the documents, and read them slowly and attentively. Then with a few eager and low-spoken words, he handed them to his companions. They perused them in turn, and seemed impressed by the contents.

"Most satisfactory indeed!" commented Baron Steuben.

"And highly important," added General Knox. "But the papers have been wet."

"Yes, I observed that they were damp," said

Washington. "How do you account for that, Master Stanbury? Why, my lad, you have surely been wet yourself! Am I not right?"

"You are right, sir," replied Nathan; and in a modest way he went on to tell of his experiences. But Washington and his companions, perceiving that more lay beneath the surface, asked question after question. Thus, by degrees, the whole of the lad's story was drawn from him, and his hearers learned in detail of the thrilling fight at the Indian Queen and the subsequent perilous escape from the town.

Washington's look was more eloquent than words, and he impulsively clasped Nathan's hand. "My brave lad!" he exclaimed, "I am proud of you. Thank God that you came safely through such terrible dangers! I have not in my army a man who could have done better."

"Not one, General!" assented Baron Steuben. "There is not one with a shrewder head and a pluckier heart."

"The lad is a hero," cried General Knox.

4

"I predict that he will be heard of in the future."

Nathan blushed at these outspoken tributes of praise. He had never known such a happy moment, and he felt more than repaid for all he had suffered.

"My lad," said Washington, "I thank you in the name of the country. You have performed a great service, and the safe-keeping of these dispatches means more than you can understand. Had they been captured by the enemy, many lives must have been forfeited. And what will you do now? You dare not return to Philadelphia at present."

"Sir, I wish to be a soldier," Nathan answered. "That is my desire above all things. But my father will not permit me to enlist."

"You will make a good soldier," declared Washington, after a thoughtful pause. "No doubt an officer in time. We have need of such recruits." He summoned an aid from the adjoining room, and said to him : "Tell Captain Stanbury that I wish to see him at once."

The man departed on his errand, and, during the interval of waiting, Nathan was made to sit down at the table, and satisfy his keen hunger on the breakfast prepared for Washington and his guests. Nathan's father presently arrived —a big, handsome man, bronzed and bearded. He warmly embraced the lad, and listened with mingled pride and alarm to the narrative of his adventurous journey.

"You have a noble son, Captain Stanbury," said Washington. "One that you may well be proud of. He tells me that his dearest wish is to serve his country in the field."

Nathan fairly trembled with eagerness and suspense, and his father looked soberly at the floor, evidently at a loss for a reply.

"Sir," he said, finally, "this is a hard thing you ask. The lad is young, and his education is still unfinished. And he is all I have in the world."

"He has proved himself a man in discretion and bravery," replied Washington. "After the events of last night it will not be safe for him to return to Philadelphia at present. And his country needs him—"

"His country shall have him, sir," cried Captain Stanbury. "Take the boy! I can no longer withhold my consent."

So the question was settled to Nathan's satisfaction and delight, and in all the camp that morning there was no heart so light and happy as his. That he had attained his dearest and long-wished-for ambition seemed almost too good to be true, and it is to be feared that he felt but slight regrets at leaving his studies and the protecting care and home of Cornelius De Vries.

He did not find an opportunity to tell his father of the mysterious visit of Mr. Noah Waxpenny to the Indian Queen, for Captain Stanbury and a small force of soldiers speedily and secretly left camp in the direction of Philadelphia, no doubt on account of the dispatches received from Anthony Benezet. And they took with them the mare and pistols borrowed from the loyal farmer.

That same morning Nathan was mustered as a private into his father's company of Wyoming men, most of whom were neighbors he had known up at his old home on the Susquehanna, and which belonged to General Mifflin's division of the Pennsylvania troops. A supply of powder and ball and a musket were given to him; but he retained his own clothes, for uniforms were few and far ,between in the American army at that time. Having thus become a full-fledged soldier the exhausted lad went to bed in the hut assigned to him, and slept under blankets all the afternoon and through the following night.

On turning out in the morning, hungry and refreshed, Nathan found a sad and shocking piece of news awaiting him. Briefly, it was as follows :

Late on the previous afternoon Captain Stanbury's little force met and attacked, midway between Valley Forge and Philadelphia, a foraging party of British soldiers in charge of two wagon-loads of provisions. In the fight that ensued the enemy were driven off with severe losses, and the supplies fell into the hands of the Americans. Only two of the latter were killed, and Captain Stanbury was shot in the groin. His men had brought him back during the night, and he was now lying in the hospital.

Thither Nathan posted in haste, only to learn from the attendants that his father was too ill to be seen, and that his ultimate recovery was very doubtful. A kind-hearted surgeon came out and tried to cheer the lad up, bidding him hope for the best; but in spite of this well-meant consolation the young recruit spent an utterly wretched day. During the morning and part of the afternoon he was under the tuition of a drill-sergeant. At another time he would have taken keen delight in learning the duties of a soldier, but the thought of his father lying in the dreary hospital made the work irksome to him, and it was a great relief when he was set at liberty.

At eventide, when supper was over, and the camp-fires were casting ruddy gleams on the quiet waters of the Schuylkill and the brown hills, Nathan was drawn aside by a member of the company named Barnabas Otter. The latter had been a friend and neighbor of Captain Stanbury and his son up at Wyoming, and though now quite an old man he was as rugged and able-bodied as many who were half his age.

"Sit down here, my boy," said Barnabas, indicating a log in front of his hut.

"None of my mess-mates are about, an' we can have a quiet chat to ourselves. This open sort of weather is nice after what we've had, but I'm thinkin' it won't last long. Lucky for you the Schuylkill wasn't froze night before last, else you would hardly have given the British troopers the slip. Why, it's the talk of the camp, lad—the way you outwitted the enemy. We fellows from Wyoming ain't the ones to be caught napping, are we?"

Nathan smiled sadly. "I did my duty, that was all," he replied. "But I would go back this minute and surrender myself to the British, if that would restore my father to health."

"I don't wonder you feel bad about it," said Barnabas. "We all do, lad, for there ain't a braver and better liked man at Valley Forge than Captain Stanbury. I only wish I'd been along to take part in that little scrimmage; it was this pesky lame foot that kept me in camp. How is the captain this evening? Have you heard?"

"Just the same—no better," answered Nathan. "I was at the hospital a bit ago, and they won't let me see him. The surgeons were awfully kind, but they don't seem to have much hope. The wound is a bad one, and it's in a vital place. Oh! what will I do if my father dies—"

The lad broke down, and could say no more. He covered his face with both hands, and hot tears fell from between his fingers.

Barnabas patted Nathan on the shoulder. "Now, now, don't take on so," he muttered huskily. "Cheer up, young comrade! Your father ain't going to die—his country and General Washington need him too badly. He's been through too much this winter to be taken

off by a British bullet. Mark my words, lad,
he'll be on his feet again before the spring campaign opens."

"I hope and pray that he will," said Nathan, cheered by the old man's confident words.

"That's the way to talk," exclaimed Barnabas. "Listen, now, an' I'll tell you what the captain an' the rest of us have been through since we went into camp here. I reckon you ain't heard all."

"I never heard as much as I wanted to," replied Nathan ; "I didn't get the chance. But I know it was awful."

"Awful ain't half the truth," declared Barnabas, with strong emphasis. "There's been wars and wars in this world, but I don't believe any army ever suffered like ours did the last few weeks. It's bad enough now, but it's not what it was. I tell you, lad, we've got to win if there's a Providence up yonder—and I know there is."

Barnabas was silent for a moment, and then he resumed. "It was the 11th of last December when we started for here from Whitmarsh, lad, and the march took us four days. Half of us were without shoes, and there was a steady trail of frozen blood along the way. And when we got here things looked as blue as could be. The place was a lonely wilderness—mostly trees and water and hills. But Washington and his officers declared it was a strong position, an' I reckon they were right."

"What did you do first?" asked Nathan.

"Built redoubts and dug entrenchments," replied Barnabas, "an' then we commenced on the huts. What a time we had of it in the bitter weather and snow, felling and hauling the trees and putting the logs together! And it took purty near as long to stuff the cracks with clay, and cover the window openings with oiled paper. Why, it was the first of the year till we got into the huts."

"I don't see how you lived through the exposure, all the time you were working and sleeping without shelter," said Nathan.

"I hardly see myself, lad, looking back on it

now," declared Barnabas. "It were little short of a miracle. We were without proper food and clothing, to say nothing of shelter. Flour and water, baked at open fires, was mostly all we had to eat, and we were without bread for days at a time. You see, supplies were scarce in the surrounding country, owin' to the military operations of last summer. Lots of us had no shirts, and the hospitals were full of barefooted soldiers who couldn't work for want of shoes."

"And where did you sleep at nights?" inquired Nathan.

"Where we could," Barnabas answered bitterly. "Those of us who had blankets were glad to sleep on the hard ground, though the weather was the coldest and the snows the deepest I ever knew. As for those who had no covering—why, lad, I've seen dozens of men, after working hard all day, sit awake around the fires from sunset till sunrise to keep from freezing. And all this time Lord Howe and his army were snug and warm in our Philadelphia, an' livin' off the fat of the land."

"Which they're doing yet," Nathan exclaimed, wrathfully. "Haven't I seen them with my own eyes?"

"Just wait till the winter's over," said Barnabas. "They may be singing a different tune then. Ain't Benjamin Franklin across the sea tryin' to get the French to help us, lad?"

"Yes," assented Nathan.

"And is there no word from him yet?"

"Not yet, Barnabas; but it may come any day."

"It can't come too soon," replied the old man. "And now to go on with my story. As I was saying, lad, it was the first of the year till we got into the huts, and since then we've been sufferin' purty near as bad. The horses died by hundreds, and the men had to haul their own supplies and fire-wood. And look at the sick men in the hospital, and men with legs amputated, and men with legs froze black—that's on account of there being no straw to sleep on. But it's no use my tellin' you, for you'll see it all yourself."

"I have seen it," exclaimed Nathan, "even in the short time I have been here, and what I wonder at most is the way the men endure their sufferings. There is no complaining—"

"Complaining?" interrupted Barnabas. "I should say not, lad. This is an army of heroes, from General Washington down. You should have seen your father during some of them blackest times, not thinking of himself, but sharing his rations and blanket with others, and helping weak and sick soldiers in their work—"

Barnabas stopped thus abruptly, seeing tears in Nathan's eyes, and wisely tacked off on a different subject. For some time longer the two friends chatted, discussing the past and the future, and deploring the well-known fact that Congress and the people were withholding their sympathies and confidence from Washington in this the darkest period of his career.

At last the bugles sounded taps, and they retired to their damp huts to sleep till the dawn of another day.

CHAPTER IV

IN WHICH NATHAN'S MILITARY CAREER VERY NEARLY TERMINATES

WITHIN a few days Nathan was thoroughly accustomed to his new life, and though the weather turned bitter and freezing, giving him a taste of the hardships the army had endured before his arrival, he felt no longing or desire to return to the comfortable guardianship of Cornelius De Vries.

On the contrary, he took pride in showing that he could endure the rigors and duties of camp-life as unflinchingly as the older and veteran soldiers. His pluck and boyish good nature quickly made him a favorite with officers and men alike. He was always ready to help a comrade, or to assume tasks that did not properly belong to him. Without a murmur he did picket-duty by day or night, in rain and snow and freezing cold. He made light of the

62

poor and scanty food that was served out to him, and when he lay awake shivering for want of sufficient covering, his bed-fellows heard never a word of complaint from his lips.

Thus a week passed, and the lad's heroic and steadfast performance of duty was all the more praiseworthy because he was hourly tortured by fears for his father's life. The result of Captain Stanbury's wound was still uncertain. He was delirious and in a high fever, and none but the hospital attendants and surgeons were permitted to see him. He was receiving the best care and treatment possible under the circumstances, and his vigorous constitution was a strong point in his favor; but until the crisis was reached the issue could not be foretold. Not only the Wyoming men, but many others as well, longed and prayed for the gallant captain's recovery. Washington sent twice daily to inquire for him, and on several occasions spoke a few words of comfort and hope to Nathan in person.

In the meantime the lad had written to Cornelius De Vries, and the letter, together with certain official dispatches to patriot friends in Philadelphia, was delivered by a trusty messenger. The latter, on his return to camp, brought papers for Washington and a reply to Nathan's letter. Of necessity the worthy Hollander wrote briefly, yet what he had to say was full of interest. He expressed deep sorrow for Captain Stanbury's critical illness, and while he showed that he was sorry to lose Nathan and missed him greatly, he took pains to give the lad some good advice suitable for a soldier's career. Referring to the memorable night at the Indian Queen, he stated that Anthony Benezet and Timothy Matlack had escaped to the lower floor of the tavern in the darkness and confusion that followed the pursuit of Nathan, and that Jenkins had concealed them in the cellar until the danger was over. "Major Langdon was slightly wounded in the arm," a postscript added, "by the bullet that shattered his lantern."

A few words must be said here concerning Mr. Noah Waxpenny. That peculiar individual did not appear again at the Indian Queen. Being under the impression that the information given him was true, and that Major Langdon was not in the town, he took up temporary quarters at the Cross Keys Inn on Chestnut Street. For several days he was occupied in making sly inquiries about Richard Stanbury and a certain other person, with what success will appear further on in the story. Then, still taking it for granted that Major Langdon was not in Philadelphia, he set out for Long Island in search of him. But on reaching New York he was prostrated by illness resulting from a heavy cold, and in that city he lay on his back for weeks, unable to give any attention to the task that had brought him to America.

A few days after the receipt of Cornelius De Vries's letter, and while Captain Stanbury was still hovering between life and death, Nathan met with an adventure which very nearly terminated fatally, but which raised him even higher in the estimation of the commander-in-chief. To his own quick wits and courage he

5

owed his escape, but in after life he could never recall that night without a shudder.

Driven by necessity to make use of a power granted him by Congress, Washington had issued a proclamation to all the farmers within seventy miles of Valley Forge—they were mostly Tories in their sympathies—ordering them to thresh out as much grain as might be demanded, and at short notice, under penalty of having their whole stock seized as straw. Requisitions were first made on the farmers living at a distance, while those in the vicinity of the camp were prudently left till the last. Among the latter was a certain Jacob Troup, a man known to be loyal to the Americans, and the owner of a large barn stocked with the previous summer's crop of wheat and oats. His turn came during the third week in February, and as the farm was close to camp, and Troup had three or four hirelings in his employ, a lot of confiscated grain was brought there to be threshed at the same time with his own.

For three days the work went on, the greater

portion of the grain accumulating in the loyal farmer's granary preparatory to being carted to camp. But, late in the afternoon of the fourth day, Washington received word that a force of British cavalry had been seen within twenty miles of Valley Forge, and this news, considered in connection with a well-founded rumor that spies were, or had been, within the lines, led him to take prompt measures to secure the large store of grain.

For this duty twenty men of the Wyoming Company were detailed, and Barnabas Otter and Nathan were of the number. So many of the officers were sick or disabled that the command of the little party fell to the lot of Corporal Dubbs. Shortly after supper they formed in the company street and marched quietly through the camp, heading southwest toward Philadelphia. They passed out of the lines between Knox's batteries and Woodford's redoubt, from which point the farmhouse of Jacob Troup was rather more than a mile distant.

It was as bitter and stormy a night as the

army at Valley Forge could remember in all that winter. That morning a brief thaw had been succeeded by a cold snap, which formed a hard crust on the snow that thickly covered the ground. Since afternoon fresh snow had been falling, and now the flakes were coming down in a dense, fine mass. Aided by a cutting wind drifts were gathering here and there, and it was impossible to see more than a few yards in any direction. The cold was still intense.

Under these circumstances the thinly-clad and poorly-shod men suffered greatly as they marched on in the teeth of the storm, leading with them four horses that were to haul the grain to camp in the farmer's big sledge. But not a word of complaint was uttered. The thought that the success of their mission meant bread for the army kept their spirits up, and like true heroes they faced the cold and snow. No doubt the brave fellows longed for a fight to heat their blood, but there was little chance that any of the British would be hovering near on such a night as this.

On they went, holding their musket-stocks with numbed fingers. In a black line they straggled through the storm, up hill and down, across patches of timber and low scrub, now knee-deep in fresh snow-drifts, now plodding over the wind-swept crust beneath. At last the leader gave the word to halt. It was in a hollow partly sheltered from the wind, and straight ahead, toward Philadelphia, the snowy landscape merged duskily into the night. To the left a narrow lane led fifty yards to the farm buildings of Jacob Troup. Word of the coming had been sent to him, and a cheery light was flashing in house and barn.

"All's well," declared Corporal Dubbs. "I expected nothing else, for the Britishers ain't the kind of chaps to stir from their warm fires in such weather. But precautions won't go amiss, and I'm going to post half a dozen pickets to watch while the rest of us load the grain."

Accordingly he selected two men, and gave them orders to advance to the left and take their stand on a road that lay some distance to the rear of the farm buildings. "Amos Brown," he said, "you and Tom Relyea march in the opposite direction—off here to the right—and keep on till you come to the road that leads to the Schuylkill beyond Valley Creek."

The corporal now turned to Barnabas Otter, pointing one numbed hand straight ahead to the southwest, in a direction at right angles to those indicated to the other sentries. "Comrade, you know who lives over yonder?" he asked.

"Abner Wilkinson," replied Barnabas. "I've seen the place often. The owner is a rank Tory."

"Ay, he's said to be," admitted the corporal, "and I reckon opinion is right. He certainly looked mighty sour when we stript him of his grain and stock. Well, to proceed, just back of Abner Wilkinson's barn is a broad lane that connects further on with the main highway from Philadelphia. It's bordered by woods, and if the enemy come at all, they'll likely come that way. So you post yourself on that little hill overlooking the road beyond the barn—it's not much over a quarter of a mile from here.

Nathan Stanbury will go with you as far as the orchard this side of the house, and that's where I want him to stay.   Do you understand?"

" Ay, ay, sir," assented Barnabas.

" And you, lad ?"

" Yes, I understand," said Nathan.   " I'm to mount guard at the edge of the orchard."

" Exactly; and keep an eye on the house. I'm telling you this because of the rumors about spies being in camp.   The family are living in Philadelphia, and Abner Wilkinson is said to be there too.   But I've my doubts about that, and you and Barnabas may learn something to-night if you're wide-awake."

The six pickets had stepped to the front as their names were called, and Corporal Dubbs now addressed them collectively in a few brief words. " These precautions are no more than my duty warrants," he said.   " A soldier never knows what's going to happen.   As for the posts I've assigned you to—why, I don't believe General Washington himself could improve on 'em.   If the enemy come they won't find us napping,

and there'll be plenty of time to save the grain.
In case all goes well you can leave your places
in about half an hour from the time you get
there. Should one of you discover the British
he will fire his musket, and then you must all
fall back. The report will reach us over here,
and will give us a chance to get the grain into
the lines. Now off with you, and be spry
about it."

The corporal gave the word to march, and his
fourteen men and four horses followed him down
the lane toward the farm-house. The six pickets, trudging off by twos, quickly vanished in
the darkness and the storm. Side by side
Nathan and Barnabas struck over the open field,
and a tramp of a quarter of a mile brought
them to the crest of a slight ridge, from whence
they saw the Tory farmer's house and barn
looming mistily out of the snow at a distance of
four hundred yards. The wind now had a clean
sweep at them, and the snow cut their faces like
sleet as they pushed on down the slope. They
felt their limbs growing numb, and half of the

time they had to close their eyes. At length, panting and exhausted, they reached the welcome shelter of the orchard, and were out of the worst of the storm. For several minutes they crouched in a snow-drift on the farther side of the fence to recover breath and to reconnoiter. But there was no sign of danger—so far as they could see or hear. The house, looming close by, had a dreary and desolate look with its shuttered windows below and its black squares of glass above.

"I reckon there's nobody in yonder," said Barnabas, his teeth chattering as he spoke. "I sort of agreed with the corporal that Abner Wilkinson might be lurking about, but I daresay he's keeping snug in Philadelphia."

"Yes, that's more likely," assented Nathan. "And I don't believe that troop of cavalry is anywhere near."

"Perhaps not," replied Barnabas, "but if they are, it'll fall to my lot to spy 'em. I must be going now, lad. Just you stay right here, and be sure to keep moving a bit, else you'll get

numbed and drop over asleep in the snow. If
you hear the crack of my weapon don't wait—
cut and run for Troup's place."

"And if I fire you'll hurry this way?" asked
Nathan.

"Of course, lad; but there's no danger of you
givin' an alarm. If the British are prowlin'
about I'll be the first to see 'em."

With this Barnabas shouldered his musket
and trudged off. His tall figure grew dimmer
and dimmer amid the flurrying snow-flakes, and
he was out of sight before he had reached the
farther end of the orchard.

A sudden feeling of loneliness now oppressed
Nathan, and with it came an unaccountable suspicion of danger. He looked warily up the
bare, white hillside toward the Troup farm, and
then he trudged across the orchard in the opposite direction. Looking from the fence past the
end of the barn, he could vaguely make out
against the sky-line the rounded and wooded
little hill on top of which Barnabas was to
mount guard. It was very nearly a quarter of

a mile distant. Coming back to his former post,
he riveted his eyes on the house. It faced toward the barn, and the side wall was directly
opposite him, separated by a thirty foot strip of
yard. He half expected to see one of the shutters thrown open, or to hear the sound of voices
from within.

But, as the minutes slipped by, and only the
moaning of the wind broke the silence of the
night, the lad grew ashamed of his fears. The
bitter cold was the only enemy he had to con-
tend with. His bare ears and hands pained
him terribly, and a slight sensation of drowsiness warned him that he must keep moving. So
he stood his musket against a big apple tree,
wrapping a rag around the flint and pan to protect them from the damp, and began to pace up
and down the narrow angle of the orchard. He
continued this for a quarter of an hour, stopping
occasionally to look and listen, until his feet had
trodden a well-defined path between the trees.
Feeling the need of more violent exercise, he
rapidly folded and unfolded his arms for a few

minutes, and then, fastening his hands on a big limb overhead, he repeatedly drew his chin up to a level with it. When he had warmed himself comfortably by these means he shouldered his musket and stepped to the fence.

"Why don't Barnabas come?" he said half aloud. "I've surely been here half an hour, and that was the limit. By this time the grain ought to be all loaded and on the way to camp. I wouldn't mind the cold if there was any fighting going on, but this sentry duty in winter is the worst part of a soldier's life. And I am anxious to get back to see how my father is—"

The sentence was stifled on the lad's lips, and he very nearly uttered a sharp cry. For just then, under one of the shuttered windows of the house, he saw a flash of yellow light. It was visible for a few seconds, and then it vanished as mysteriously as it had appeared.

Nathan felt a cold shiver run down his back. "Did I imagine that light?" he asked himself, " or is there some one in the house?"

The next instant he was crouching low behind

the fence, every nerve quivering with excitement, and his musket trembling in his hands. He had made another startling discovery, and one that was too real to be doubted. The dark figure of a man was approaching the rear of the house from the direction of the American lines, and it was only too evident that he was not one of Corporal Dubbs's sentries. On he came through the drifted snow, stepping quickly but stealthily, and turning his head from right to left.

Nathan aimed his musket through the fence. "A spy!" he muttered. "He's just been to the camp! Shall I shoot?" putting his finger to the trigger. "No, I have a better plan. He's going to the house, and there he'll be trapped."

The lad was right. A moment later the crouching figure had gained the rear wall and was lost to sight. A door was heard to softly open and close.

Nathan watched and listened in vain. For half a minute he hesitated. Should he hurry off to bring Barnabas, or should he first endeavor to learn who was in the house? The thought that he might, after all, be mistaken decided him. Holding his musket ready for instant use he lightly scaled the fence, and waded through the snow to the side wall of the house. He crept to the rear angle, cautiously peeped around, and then boldly turned it. A few steps brought him to the door, and he discovered it was open a few inches. The wind had evidently done this, the latch having failed to drop into its socket.

Nathan stood at attention, outwardly cool and alert in spite of his inward excitement. All was black behind the crevice, but he could hear faint voices at a distance. The temptation was too strong to be resisted, and with a sudden impulse he carefully pushed the door farther open and stepped into what seemed to be a wide hall. Looking to the left he saw another door. This also was open an inch or two, and in the lighted room to which it led two persons were talking in low and eager tones.

"I've got to find out who's in there," the lad

resolved. Holding his gun in front of him he advanced with a cat-like tread. Happily the bare floor did not creak under him, and his ragged shoes were so full of snow that they made no noise. He reached the door, halted, and peered anxiously through the crack.

What he saw was a small room, scantily furnished with a bed, two chairs, and a table. A lamp was burning dimly on a shelf, and every crevice of the one window was stuffed with rags to keep the light from showing outside—a precaution that had not been entirely successful.

In the chair beside the table sat a bearded, harsh-looking man, who could be none other than Abner Wilkinson himself; he was wrapped in a heavy cloak and held a hat in his hand. Near by stood the man who had just entered the house. He was young and smooth-shaven, with a handsome but sinister countenance. He was hurriedly exchanging his snowy and wet garments for a uniform of green faced with white—the uniform, as Nathan well knew, of the Tory soldiers of the British army.

The lad saw all this at a brief glance, and then he listened keenly to the conversation. "I wouldn't have done what you did for a king's ransom," Abner Wilkinson was saying. "Man, you took your life in your hands—"

"But I got what I wanted," the other interrupted, calmly, "and now that I have them safe we had better be off at once. There's no telling what will happen if the loss is discovered, as it may be at any moment."

"It's a bad night to travel on foot," said Abner Wilkinson. "Don't you think we might wait till morning? There's no danger of your being traced here, for the snow will cover your footsteps—"

"But not right away. I tell you we're in danger, and the sooner we start the better. Have you got those other papers ready?"

"Yes, Captain," the Tory farmer answered; and he stepped toward a closet at the end of the room.

Out in the dark hall Nathan trembled with excitement. "They have papers," he said to himself, "and the one in uniform has been spying in our lines.   They musn't get away."

Just then Abner Wilkinson turned around from the closet, holding a packet in his hand. "Here they are, Captain," he said.

"Put them in your pocket," replied the officer. "They may be as important as those I have. Are you ready to start? We'll go as soon as Mawhood comes back. I'm beginning to feel worried about him."

"Oh, he'll be in presently," said Wilkinson, "unless he's lost his bearings in the storm—"

Nathan trembled with sudden fear, missing the rest of the sentence. "There's another spy," he reflected, "and he's outside somewhere. These two are waiting for him. Whew! what a scrape I'm in ! There's no time to lose if I want to get away."

He turned cautiously around to retreat, and even as he did so the floor creaked and he saw a dark object between himself and the outer door. The next instant, as he made a headlong dash for liberty, a strong arm encircled him and

6

a hand clutched his throat. The lad's musket fell with a crash, and he struggled hard to break loose. But his efforts were futile. In less time than it takes to tell he was dragged, bruised and half-choked, into the room. Abner Wilkinson was trembling with fright in a far corner, and the officer had drawn a sword and a pistol. With an oath he reached for the lamp, evidently intending to blow it out.

"Stop, sir; you needn't do that," cried Nathan's captor, who was a burly Britisher in plain dress. "There's only one of 'em, and I've got him safe. He must have crept into the house a bit ago, for he was listening at yonder door when I spied him." He released the lad's throat, and held him out at arm's length.

The officer glared at Nathan. "Are you sure there are no more, Mawhood?" he demanded hoarsely.

"Quite sure, Captain," the man replied. "There's a party of rebels removing the grain from Troup's farm back across the hill, and this chap was posted here as an advance picket.

There are no others in the neighborhood, for I've been all around the house. But I would advise getting away just as quick as possible—"

"Yes, yes, let's start at once!" interrupted Abner Wilkinson, who was pale with fright. "We will be hung if we are caught."

"We must attend to the prisoner first," said the officer. "Who are you?" he added to the lad. "Why did you come in here?"

Nathan tightened his lips and made no reply.

"Do you hear?" thundered the officer. "Answer my questions! Were you listening at the door while we talked? Are any more of your rebel friends posted in the neighborhood?"

"I won't tell you, sir," the lad replied firmly.

"You won't?" cried the officer. "Well, if you did it wouldn't help you any now. I'm going to hang you, my fine fellow."

"Yes, hang the dog," exclaimed the Tory farmer. "I'll show you how." He darted to the closet and produced a coil of heavy rope. The soldier quickly seized this in obedience to a signal from his officer, threw one end over a thick beam of the ceiling, and deftly looped the other end. Swish! the fatal noose settled on Nathan's neck, and was tightened by a jerk.

The lad stood firm, but in a few seconds a thousand thoughts seemed to flit through his throbbing brain. He thought of Philadelphia, of Cornelius De Vries, of his father lying sick in the hospital—of all his past life. He realized that there was no hope for him. Even should he shout, Barnabas and the other sentries were too far away to hear him.

Mawhood stood face to face with Nathan at a distance of a couple of feet. The end of the rope was twisted in both his hands, and the officer was close alongside of him. The latter pulled out a watch. "I'll give you twenty seconds to pray," he said, "and then up you go."

"Don't murder me," Nathan begged hoarsely. "I've done nothing to deserve death."

"You're a dog of a rebel," was the brutal answer, "and that's enough. Ten seconds gone."

The lad glanced at the mocking and merciless faces of his enemies, hardly realizing his doom, and then a ray of hope flashed suddenly to his bewildered brain. His hands had fortunately been left untied, and as he saw a huge pistol protruding from the soldier's belt decision and action were almost simultaneous. A rapid snatch, and the barrel of the weapon was between his fingers. As quickly the butt crushed with stunning force on Mawhood's temple, and over he went like a log, the rope slipping from his nerveless fingers.

Back Nathan sprang with a shout, and reversing and cocking the pistol he turned it on the officer. The latter already had his own pistol out and leveled, but when the hammer fell only a sharp click followed. With an oath he dodged to one side, and his agility saved his life. The lad's bullet barely grazed him, and struck Abner Wilkinson, who was directly in range. With a shrill cry the Tory farmer fell to his knees and then toppled over on his back.

The report was terrific and seemed to shake the very house. The powder smoke hid the

scene for a moment, and then it cleared sufficiently to reveal the officer in the act of drawing
his sword. There was no time to hesitate, and
Nathan dashed at him before he could lift the
weapon for a thrust. The two grappled, swayed
fiercely for a few moments, and then came
heavily to the floor. Over and over they rolled
in a tight embrace, the officer cursing most
savagely, and Nathan shouting at the top of his
voice.

The struggle lasted but a short time, though
to the combatants it seemed a long while. The
lad was the weaker of the two, and he realized
that he must soon succumb. But he fought on,
gasping hard for breath, and just when his hold
was relaxing there came a rush of feet and a
loud shout.

The faithful Barnabas had arrived, and without an instant's delay he hauled the officer away
from his intended victim. Nathan was able to
assist, and between the two the desperate Britisher was overpowered and his arms were bound
behind him with the rope that had so nearly

ended the plucky lad's life. Abner Wilkinson
was just breathing his last, and the soldier Mawhood was beginning to show signs of returning
consciousness.

"The shot brought me here in time," exclaimed Barnabas. "But what does it all mean,
lad?"

Before Nathan could reply a muffled clatter
of hoofs was heard from the rear of the house,
followed by the shrill whinny of a horse. Barnabas and the lad exchanged startled glances,
but they quickly discovered that they had no
cause for alarm. The next instant half a dozen
soldiers in the uniform of Washington's body-
guard surged into the room, and with them,
muffled in a heavy cloak, was General Washington himself.

"Gentlemen, we appear to have come too late,"
remarked the commander-in-chief. "I think
that is the spy yonder." Then he asked for
explanations, and Nathan briefly and clearly told
the whole story.

"You have done well," said Washington.

"Search that man at once," he added, pointing to the prisoner.

Barnabas did so, and speedily produced a thick bundle of papers. Washington took them eagerly, glanced over them, and then thrust them into his bosom.

"These were stolen from a chest in my private room but half an hour ago," he said. "The thief entered the window by means of a tree, and I suppose the storm enabled him to pass the sentries. Fortunately the loss was discovered a few moments afterward, and before the snow had covered the man's tracks sufficiently to prevent us from following him. The importance and value of the papers cannot be exaggerated, and I am indeed fortunate to recover them."

Washington now ordered Abner Wilkinson to be searched. The Tory was quite dead, having been shot through the heart, and in his pocket were found minute plans and data relating to the camp, showing that the man must have made numerous excursions within the lines.

As there was possible danger of a surprise by

British cavalry, the whole party speedily left the house, taking the two prisoners with them, but leaving the body of the Tory behind. Mawhood and the officer refused to speak, and they sullenly submitted to be mounted behind a couple of the troopers. Barnabas and Nathan trudged behind the little procession to the house of Jacob Troup, where they found Corporal Dubbs and his men in a state of excitement induced by the pistol shot. The other sentries had come in, and the grain was already far on its way to camp. An hour later all who had participated in the night's adventure were sleeping soundly in their quarters, and the two prisoners were pacing restlessly up and down the narrow confines of the guard-house, with the spectre of the hangman's noose dangling over them.

The following day Nathan was summoned to headquarters, where Washington thanked him for the great service he had performed and complimented him highly on his pluck and bravery. This gave the lad keen pleasure, but it was as nothing compared to the joy he felt a week later, when his father passed the crisis and began to recover. His convalescence lasted a long time, and during that period Nathan did not venture to excite or worry his father by telling him of the visit of Mr. Noah Waxpenny to the Indian Queen. And when at last Captain Stanbury had entirely recovered, the lad had come to regard the affair as hardly worth speaking of.

Brief mention must be made of the two men captured in the farm-house of Abner Wilkinson. The officer turned out to be Captain Conway, of the Tory troop of horse known as the Queen's Rangers, and Mawhood was a private of the same force. Death by hanging would certainly have been their punishment had they not made a desperate attempt to escape shortly before being brought to trial. Mawhood did succeed in eluding the guards and getting out of the camp, but Captain Conway was riddled with musket-balls and killed instantly.

CHAPTER V

IN WHICH BEGINS A MEMORABLE BATTLE

As the spring months wore on, bringing sunshine and warmth instead of snow and ice, the situation at Valley Forge changed decidedly for the better. The shadows of the winter were fading before the hopes of freedom promised by the fresh campaign soon to be opened. Most of the sick had recovered, and the troops fit for active service numbered about fifteen thousand. They had much to cheer them, and the greatest source of gratification was the good news from France. For, early in February, Benjamin Franklin had negotiated a treaty with that nation, news of which reached the United States in the following May, and was promptly ratified by Congress. And, to further encourage the struggling people, it was learned that a French fleet, commanded by Count d'Estaing, had already sailed for Philadelphia.

Meanwhile, on the 11th of May, Lord Howe had been superseded in command of the British army by Sir Henry Clinton, and it was generally believed that the latter had been ordered by the ministry to evacuate Philadelphia.

But that much-desired event was long delayed. The enemy spent weeks in slothful preparation, and the middle of June found the boats of the fleet all collected and moored below the town— which was taken as a pretty sure sign that the flight would be by water. At almost any day the French armament might be expected to sail up the Delaware.

But, in spite of this danger of a blockade, the British still lingered, to the satisfaction of Tory citizens and the disgust of all good patriots. And at Valley Forge, Washington was patiently watching and waiting, with his orders written out, his baggage ready to be packed at a moment's notice, and his troops in condition to form in line of march at the first beat of the drum.

It was past midday of the 17th of June, 1778,

when the long-expected word came at last to the American camp. It was in the form of a private dispatch, the tenor of which was not at once communicated to the army. But a conference took place between Washington and his staff, as a result of which a trusty officer named Captain McLane left Valley Forge that evening under secret orders. He was suitably disguised and well mounted.

The night was far advanced when Captain McLane entered Philadelphia, unchallenged by a single sentry as he rode along.

He found the town in a ferment of excitement and joy. At nine o'clock the long-expected evacuation of the British army had begun. Down to the Delaware the troops marched quietly, regiment by regiment, and embarked in small boats. But instead of boarding the big vessels at anchor, they crossed the river and disembarked on the Jersey shore. The retreat was to be by land, and not by water.

Captain McLane found means of crossing with the enemy, and all night long, while the boats flitted from shore to shore, the brave man went here and there unsuspected. He followed the lead of the column five miles into the Jersies, to Haddonfield, ascertained General Clinton's intended line of march, and then retraced his steps past the long train of baggage, provisions, carriages, and saddle-horses that brought up the rear of the retreating army.

He safely reached the city early on the morning of the 18th—while the evacuation was still in progress—and before ten o'clock he was back at the camp with the electrifying news. Two hours after the last of the British had departed, Washington's dragoons were riding through the streets of Philadelphia, and a small detachment under General Arnold occupied the town.

Before night the whole of the patriot army was in motion toward the Delaware, and the huts at Valley Forge, consecrated by the winter's heroic sufferings and fortitude, were left to solitude and decay. The line of march was in the direction of Trenton, it being the intention of Washington to press closely on the rear of the enemy, and of the thousands of American soldiers who longed for a decisive battle, none desired it more ardently than Nathan Stanbury and his father.

General Clinton led the British army northeast through the Jersies, his object being to reach the Raritan River and there embark his troops. But the sandy roads and oppressively hot weather made marching tedious and slow, and, as there was but a single road, his train of baggage-wagons, horses and men made a line nearly twelve miles in extent. In addition, he had to build bridges and causeways over the streams and marshes.

Meanwhile the American army was moving swiftly, and had crossed the Delaware near Trenton in several divisions. On the 25th of June, learning that Washington was almost on his front, Clinton concluded to change his course rather than risk a general action with his numerous encumbrances. So, turning to the right, he followed the road leading to Monmouth Court-house and Sandy Hook, intending now to embark his troops at the latter place instead of on the Raritan.

As yet Washington was himself disinclined to risk a battle, and was merely trying to harass the enemy on their march. The advance American forces—certain corps and brigades under Maxwell, Morgan, Scott, Dickinson, and Cadwallader—had been ordered to annoy the British on the rear and flanks. On June 25th, when Clinton turned toward Monmouth Court-house, the Americans reached a place called Kingston. Here another council was held, and though General Lee, as before, was strongly opposed to any interference with the movements of the enemy, Lafayette, Green, and Wayne declared in favor of a general battle. Washington was of the same mind, and so he promptly proceeded to make his arrangements to that effect. He sent a thousand men forward under General Wayne to join the troops nearest the enemy, gave Lafayette the command of all the advanced forces, and himself moved with the main body to Cranberry on the 28th of June.

Early on the morning of the 27th, Lafayette reached Englishtown, a village about five miles to the west of Monmouth Court-house. The British general, being advised of the movements of the Americans, prepared for battle at Monmouth, where he had now arrived. He placed his baggage train in front and his best troops— the grenadiers, light infantry, and chasseurs—in the rear. Then he encamped near the Court-house, in a strong position that was secured by woods and marshy ground. His line stretched a mile and a half on the right toward Shrewsbury, and three miles on the left in the direction of Allentown.

Washington heard of this, and found it necessary to increase the numbers of his advance corps. He sent Lee with two brigades to join Lafayette, and gave him the command of the whole division. The main army marched the same day to within three miles of Englishtown. Morgan was now hovering on the British right, and a force of militia under Dickinson was menacing their left. Three miles beyond

7

Monmouth were the heights of Middletown, which offered a great advantage to the enemy. To prevent them from obtaining that advantage, Washington determined to attack their rear the moment they should attempt to move, and he gave General Lee orders to that effect. Sir Henry Clinton, finding a battle to be inevitable, was no less busy, and the night of the 27th was one of anxiety to both armies.

The 28th of June, 1778, was Sunday. The sun rose out of a cloudless sky, and not a breath of air was stirring. It was the hottest and sultriest day of the year. The Americans were all eager for the fight, and hopeful of striking a decisive blow at the enemies of their country. The force to which Nathan and the Wyoming men belonged were with the main army back near Englishtown, and this was a disappointment to the lad, since he feared that he would miss the battle. But his anxiety was needless, as after events proved.

Before dawn the regiment of Colonel Grayson and the brigades of Scott and Varnum were in the saddle and moving toward Monmouth Court-house. General Knyphausen, with a British force that comprised Hessians and Pennsylvania and Maryland Tories, advanced at daybreak, followed later by Sir Henry Clinton with his main army. Dickinson, observing the earlier movement, sent an express in haste to Lee and the commander-in-chief. Washington at once put his army in motion, and sent orders to General Lee to attack the enemy unless there should be a strong reason to the contrary.

So Lee pressed forward, supported by Dickinson, Grayson, and the brigades of Wayne and Maxwell. He crossed the morass by a causeway near the parsonage, and on reaching a height was joined by Lafayette with the main body of the advanced corps. Here conflicting intelligence was received, some messengers asserting that the enemy were in full retreat, while others reported that the whole British army was filing off to the right to attack the Americans.

Satisfied that no important bodies of foes were on either of his flanks, Lee marched on with about five thousand troops through a broken and heavily-wooded country, and came to the verge of the plain of Monmouth. Seeing a column of the British about two thousand strong on the left, and taking them to be a covering party, he determined to try to cut them off from the main army. So he sent Wayne with artillery and seven hundred men to attack them in the rear, while he himself sought to gain their front by a short cut.

It was now nine o'clock in the morning. Wayne was about to descend on the enemy when a body of the Queen's Dragoons appeared on the edge of a wood, parading as though about to make an attack. Lee, seeing this, planned and partly carried out a clever ruse. He ordered his light horse to entice the dragoons as near as possible, and then retreat to Wayne's position. The dragoons, following the light horse as was expected, were met with a hot musketry fire from an ambush party under Colonel Butler, of Wayne's command. Then they wheeled about and galloped off toward the main column.

Wayne ordered Colonel Oswald to open two pieces of artillery upon them, and he himself made a bayonet charge forward with his whole force.

The battle now seemed about to begin in earnest, for Wayne and his command were fighting with vigor, and with good prospect of success. He was therefore greatly chagrined and irritated when Lee ordered him to make only a feigned attack, lest he (Lee) should fail in his plan to cut off the covering party. But Wayne was a true soldier. He obeyed without questioning and checked his troops, hoping that Lee would recover what his untimely order had lost. But here again Wayne was disappointed, for only a small portion of Lee's troops issued from the wood on the right, and these were actually within cannon-shot of the royal forces.

About this time Sir Henry Clinton discovered that the Americans were marching in force on both his flanks, and with the hope of drawing them off by making an urgent necessity for them elsewhere, he faced his army around and prepared to attack Wayne. This move was made, and soon a large body of cavalry were seen approaching. Lafayette discovered this, and it suggested so good a plan to him that he rode straightway and in haste to Lee.

"General," he cried, "have I your permission to gain the rear of these cavalry who are marching against us? I am satisfied that I can do so, and thus cut them off."

"Sir, you do not knew British soldiers," replied Lee. "We cannot stand against them. We shall be driven back at first, and we must be cautious."

"Perhaps you are right, General," declared Lafayette. "But British soldiers have been beaten before this, and they are not invincible. At all events, I wish to make this attempt."

Lee partly consented, ordering Lafayette to wheel his column by the right, and gain and attack the cavalry's left. Next he unaccountably weakened Wayne's detachment on the left by sending three regiments to the right, and then rode toward Oswald's battery to reconnoiter.

At this moment, to his great astonishment, as he afterward declared, Lee saw a large portion of the British army marching on the Middletown road toward the Court-house. Apparently confused, he immediately ordered his right to fall back, and gave other commands that virtually amounted to a retreat. Lafayette was instructed to fall back to the Court-house, and Generals Maxwell and Scott, who were about to form for action on the plain, were sent to the woods in their rear.

A general and disastrous retreat had now begun, and one for which there was no excuse, since Lee might have made an effective stand in his advantageous position. The Americans were pursued as far as the Court-house, where the British temporarily halted and opened fire with several batteries. The routed army pressed on across the morass, suffering terribly from heat, thirst, and fatigue, and sinking ankle-deep in the loose and sandy soil. They reached the broken heights of Freehold, and paused here for a brief rest. But soon the British forces came on, and Lee resumed his retreat toward the Freehold meeting-house. The demoralized troops fled in great confusion, many perishing in the mud and water of the swamps, and others, dropping over with the heat, being trampled to death by those behind. It was a black commencement to the battle of Monmouth.

Meanwhile Washington had been pressing forward in haste, and with his right wing commanded by General Greene, and the left wing in charge of himself, he had reached the vicinity of the Freehold meeting-house and Monmouth Court-house. Just at that time arrived a farmer on a fleet horse, announcing that Lee and his forces were in full retreat, with the enemy in close pursuit. Washington at once rode forward with his staff, passing and checking the flying columns of troops, until he met Lee near the rear.

"Sir," he cried, in tones of bitter anger, "I desire to know whence arises this disorder and confusion, and what is the reason."

Lee was a high-spirited man, and being stung

more by the manner than the words of his commander, he retorted harshly. A few sharp words passed between the two, but there was no time for full explanations, since the advancing enemy were within fifteen minutes' march.

CHAPTER VI

WHEELING his horse, Washington spurred on toward the rear to avert the consequences of Lee's disaster and check the rout, and the effect of his personal presence on the demoralized troops was speedy and gratifying. Within ten minutes the retreat was suspended, the fugitives were rallying, and order and discipline were visible in the midst of the confusion.

Colonel Oswald, with two pieces of artillery, took a position on an eminence, and by a well-directed fire from his battery, checked the pursuing enemy. Stewart and Ramsey supported him, having formed their troops under cover of a wood. While the British grenadiers were pouring their deadly volleys into the still broken ranks of the Americans, Washington rode fearlessly to and fro in the face of the leaden storm, issuing order after order. The whole of

106

Lee's army, so shortly before on the verge of destruction, was soon drawn up in battle array, with a bold and well-arranged front. Having thus saved the day, Washington rode back to General Lee.

"Will you command in that place, sir?" he said curtly, pointing to the reformed division.

"I will," Lee answered, eagerly.

"Then I expect you to check the enemy at once."

"Your command shall be obeyed," assured Lee, "and I will not be the first to leave the field."

Washington hurried further back to the main army, and lost no time in forming it in battle order on the ridge that rose above the western side of the morass. Meanwhile General Lee partly atoned for his fault by a display of skill and courage in obedience to his commander's orders. While a hot cannonade was going on between the artillery of both forces, he gallantly repulsed a troop of royal light horse that charged upon the right of his division. Never-

theless the enemy were too strong to be held in
check more than temporarily, and before long
the greater part of the Americans were obliged
to give way and fall back toward Washington.

Stretching across the open field in front of
the causeway over the morass was a hedgerow,
and here the conflict raged for some little time,
the place being held stoutly by Livingston's
regiment and Varnum's brigade, with a battery
of artillery. But their ranks were finally broken
by a desperate bayonet charge from the British
cavalry and infantry, and Varnum and Livingston, with the artillery, retreated across the
morass, their rear effectually protected by
Colonel Ogden and his men, who held a wood
near the causeway. Lee was the last to leave
the field, bringing Ogden's corps off with him,
and after forming the whole of his division in
good order on the hillside west of the morass,
he reported to Washington for further instructions.

Lee's forces had thus far borne the brunt of
the day's fighting, so Washington considerately

ordered them to the rear in the direction of Englishtown, while he himself prepared to engage the enemy with the fresh and main army. His left was commanded by Lord Stirling, and the right by General Greene. Wayne was on an eminence in an orchard near the parsonage, while on his right a battery of artillery occupied the crest of Comb's Hill.

The battle now began in earnest, the enemy being drawn up in force on the hills and in the fields across the morass, and having possession of the lost hedgerow. They were repulsed from the American left, and on trying to turn the right flank they were driven back by Knox's battery, supported by General Greene. Meanwhile Wayne kept up a brisk fire on the British centre, and repeatedly hurled back the royal grenadiers, who several times advanced upon him from the hedgerow.

The commander of the grenadiers, Colonel Monckton, determined to make a last attempt to drive Wayne from his position. So he formed his men in solid column, and advanced anew.

with the regularity of a corps on parade. Wayne's troops were partly sheltered by a barn, and they reserved their fire until the enemy were very close. Monckton was about to give the order to charge, sword in hand, when the terrible volley was poured forth. He himself was killed instantly, and most of the British officers fell with him. A desperate hand-to-hand fight ensued, and the survivors of the grenadiers finally fled in confusion, leaving the body of their commander behind. Thus the conflict raged from point to point, while the sultry day grew older, and the roar of cannons and muskets echoed far over the peaceful Jersey countryside.

And what was Nathan Stanbury doing all this time? We shall see. Behind the American lines was the meeting-house, and in front, down the hill toward the swamp that separated the two armies, were the parsonage and barn, an orchard, and a bit of woods. These places of shelter bristled with Washington's skirmishers. From behind trees and fences, from the loopholes and crevices of the barn, they poured a hot and steady fire on the red-coats.

The Pennsylvania regiment to which the Wyoming troops belonged, occupied the strip of woods near the morass. Nathan was crouched behind a stump, and next to him was Barnabas Otter. Captain Stanbury was twenty feet away, and from time to time he looked anxiously around to see that his boy was all right. Overhead bullets whistled, sending down fluttering showers of leaves and twigs. Shells went screeching and hissing by, some bursting far off, others exploding close at hand with a deafening report. But Nathan kept his place like an old soldier, steadily loading and firing, and shifting the hot breech of his musket from hand to hand.

At first the lad was nervous under fire, but that feeling had long since passed away. His head was cool and his nerves steady. He felt that he had to do his part in winning the battle, and he regretted that his post of duty was with the skirmishers instead of on one of the flanks of the main army. Men died around him by shot and shell, but these dreadful sights only made his hand steadier and his aim truer.

" Be careful, boy," his father called to him. " Keep your head down."

"All right, sir," Nathan shouted back, " but I've got to see to fire."

"Aim low, lad," muttered old Barnabas Otter. " You know it's the·natural tendency of a musket to carry high."

"And who taught me that but yourself, Barnabas?" retorted Nathan. " Have you forgotten all the fat deer I killed up on the Susquehanna?   I'm shooting just as carefully now."

He went on loading and firing, peering this way and that through the smoke to get a glimpse of the red-coats. Far off he saw officers galloping to and fro, and he wondered if one of them could be Godfrey Spencer. He hoped the cruel fortune of war would not bring them together on the battle-field.

So, for hour after hour through the long afternoon, the fight went on, the skirmishers bravely holding their position. To right and left, where the morass ended, there was a constant panorama of moving cavalry, infantry and guns. The roar of battle echoed miles away, and the smoke floated overhead on the still air. The heat was terrific, and men dropped, fainting and exhausted, to the ground. Not since Bunker Hill had the American army shown such desperate valor. In vain Clinton thundered and stormed at the centre. In vain did Lord Cornwallis assail Sterling's invincible left wing.

The approach of evening found both armies still holding their ground, and now a large force of the British advanced on the American right wing. But a spare battery hastened to that quarter, unlimbered their guns, and poured into the enemy such a storm of shot and shell as drove them back in confusion.

Part of an infantry brigade—mostly grenadiers—passed near the strip of woods. The skirmishers had just turned their fire in this direction when a mounted officer arrived with orders to charge on the enemy's flank. With

8

ringing cheers the Pennsylvania regiment poured out from the trees, Captain Stanbury's Wyoming company in front; and a double-quick trot brought them to close quarters with the rear of the British.

The grenadiers doggedly kept up the retreat, firing as they went, and many fell on both sides. Most of the enemy's officers were far in front, and Nathan felt sure that he recognized Godfrey's figure at a distance.

But one mounted officer, seeing what was taking place, pluckily galloped back to the rear to try to rally the broken lines. He ventured too far, and a shot brought horse and rider to the ground. Before his own men could rescue him, the front line of the Americans was nearly at the spot.

Barnabas and Nathan had seen the occurrence, and they ran up to the officer just as he struggled to his feet from under the body of his horse. At the first glance Nathan recognized Major Langdon, and he was quick to observe the half healed scar on his left wrist.

"SURRENDER!" YELLED BARNABAS

"Surrender!" yelled Barnabas, presenting his musket at the officer's head.

Major Langdon glanced around, bit his lip passionately, and then dropped his half-drawn sword into its scabbard.

"The fortune of war has made me your prisoner," he said proudly; "I am an officer and a gentleman, and I demand proper treatment."

"You Britishers never were backward about demandin'," snorted Barnabas. "Fall to the rear now."

Though the bullets were flying thickly Major Langdon showed no inclination to move, he had suddenly seen and recognized Nathan, and there was a strange look of hatred on his deeply flushed face as he stared at the lad. Nathan returned the officer's piercing gaze for an instant, and then, hearing a couple of loud shouts to one side, he looked around in time to see his father toss up his arms and fall.

The retreating grenadiers were still being hotly pressed, both sides firing steadily, but half a dozen men of Captain Stanbury's company at once ran to him. He was lying on his back, deathly pale, and with blood oozing from the left breast of his coat.

He lifted himself on one elbow as Nathan reached him and sank tearfully down at his side.

"I am wounded, my boy—mortally wounded," he gasped, "but before I die I have a secret to tell you—a secret that will change your whole life. Listen, while I have breath to speak."

CHAPTER VII

IN WHICH A BUTTON BETRAYS ITS OWNER

"No, no, you will not die, father," cried Nathan. "It may not be a mortal wound. Where are you hit?" He looked wildly around, wringing his hands. "Can't something be done?" he added. "Bring water from the swamp, or send for a surgeon."

"I'm afraid it's no use, lad," said the lieutenant of the company. "If it was possible to help him—"

"No, I'm past human aid," groaned the wounded man. "My time has come, and I must answer the call. I'm shot in the breast, and my strength is nearly spent. Compose yourself, dear boy, and listen to me. Remember, it may soon be too late."

Nathan forced back the tears, and with a white, rigid face, he bent nearer his dying parent. "Speak, father," he replied, huskily. "I am listening."

Captain Stanbury nodded. "There are papers buried under the floor of my cabin up at Wyoming," he said in a voice that was broken with pain. "I have kept them all these years—for you. Get them, Nathan, and guard them carefully. You little know—how important they are."

"Yes, I will get them, father," promised Nathan.

"Barnabas will help you, lad. He is a trusty old friend—and neighbor."

"You kin count on me, Captain," declared Barnabas, as he wiped a tear from his eye with the palm of his horny hand. "An' what are you doin' here, Mister Redcoat?" he added sharply.

The last remark was addressed to Major Langdon. He had pushed into the group uninvited, and heard the American officer's words to his son. Now, as he peeped furtively at the wounded man from one side, his face was pale and bloodless under its bronzed skin, and in his black eyes was a strange and half-triumphant expression.

"Have you a prisoner there?" asked Captain Stanbury, catching a glimpse of the red uniform. "See that he is well treated, men. Oh, this pain!" he added, grasping at his breast. "Nathan—don't forget—the papers—they contain the secret—and the proofs of—" His head dropped back and his eyes closed, the secret that had been on his lips still untold.

Was the brave officer living or dead? There was no time to tell. As Nathan clasped his father's hands in a passion of grief, the straggling musketry-fire in front suddenly ceased, and back in full flight poured the Pennsylvania troops. On their right flank, sweeping along under the gathering shades of evening to cover the retreat of the British brigade, came a compact line of dragoons. A dozen voices yelled at Nathan, but he only shook his head.

"Take my father along," he cried, "and I will go."

Crack! crack! crack!—the rear ranks of the grenadiers had turned and were firing. The dragoons were galloping closer. A ball tore the lad's cap from his head, and he sprang to his feet, staring around him undecidedly. Then Barnabas Otter and Corporal Dubbs grasped him by each arm, and in spite of protest they dragged him rapidly along with the retreating regiment. In the rout Major Langdon was forgotten, and he seized the opportunity to drop into a clump of bushes, where he lay unseen until his own men came up.

The dragoons continued the pursuit almost to the edge of the woods, and there a hot fire from the rallied skirmishers, and a few shells from Knox's guns on the hillside, drove them back with severe loss to the British lines.

Night was now closing in, and with darkness the battle ended. The British had lost nearly a thousand; the Americans less than three hundred. But Washington was not satisfied. He issued orders to resume the attack at daylight,

and after eating supper in ranks the weary
troops slept upon their arms.

For Nathan the joy of victory was swallowed
up in bitter grief. After the moon rose, with Barnabas Otter and a few other faithful comrades,
he ventured out from the woods to recover his
father's body. But it could not be found,
though the spot where he had fallen was easily
located. All around were dead and wounded,
British and American, but no sign of Captain
Stanbury.

"It's no use to look," said Nathan. "My
father is not dead. He is alive, and a prisoner
in the hands of the enemy."

"What makes you think so?" asked Barnabas.

"Because the British have left their own dead
on the field," was the reply. "Would they
have carried off an American officer, unless he
was alive?"

"True fur that, lad," said Barnabas, "but
it's a mighty queer disappearance just the same."
His brow knitted as he remembered the strange
and evil look on Major Langdon's face while

he watched Captain Stanbury. "I wish that stuck-up British officer hadn't slipped away," he added angrily, little dreaming, as he spoke the words, of what the major's escape was to cost himself and others.

"We'd better be going back, my lad," said Corporal Dubbs. "Your father will be exchanged one of these days, if he is alive; and I don't doubt but he is. It's my belief the ball glanced from his ribs, or went in a bit sidewise, and whichever it was the pain and shock would be enough to make him faint."

Nathan brightened up at this opinion, and his mood was cheerful as he trudged back to the lines with the search party.

"What can those papers contain?" he asked himself. "I suppose they will reveal the secret of my father's early life, of which he would never speak. I will get them at the first chance, but I will never open them so long as there is a possibility of my father being alive. A dozen times in the past week I was tempted to tell him of the queer chap who inquired for him at the

Indian Queen.   I wish now I had done so, but it is too late for regrets."

Nathan's sleep that night was peaceful, but he awoke in the morning to share a great disappointment with the whole army. Under cover of darkness, the British had stolen off, cavalry, infantry, and batteries.   They were already miles on the march to Middletown—too far away to be overtaken.

This discovery was followed immediately by a piece of news that proved of the deepest interest to Nathan and his friends.   A courier rode into camp with a letter for Washington from the Board of War.   It appeared that messengers had lately been sent to the Board by the Wyoming settlers, stating that their peaceful valley was threatened by the invasion of a large force of Tories and Seneca Indians under Colonel John Butler; that they were too few in number to hold their scattered forts with any hope of success, and begging for the immediate return of their able-bodied men who were serving in the American army.   The letter concluded by urging that their request should be acceded to.

Washington lost not an hour's time, realizing that the intended attack was prompted by the knowledge that the greater part of the fighting men of the settlements were absent, and that it might even now be too late to save the almost defenseless women and children from Tory bullets and Indian tomahawks.

Ammunition and arms were distributed to the Wyoming men, and ere the sun was well up the little band—numbering less than ten-score—had started on their long march of nearly one hundred and fifty miles to the northwest, eager to save families and friends from massacre.

Nathan and Barnabas were naturally of the party, and while they shared the fears and resolves of the others, they were also determined to procure the papers that were buried under Captain Stanbury's cabin—the success of which mission depended on their reaching the valley before it should be seized and occupied by the enemy. General Washington had promised to do all in his power to procure the exchange of Nathan's father—if he was still alive—and this enabled the lad to set out on his journey with a comparatively light heart.

Barnabas Otter was a product of the early days of Pennsylvania colonization. One of the first settlers in the Wyoming Valley, his bravery and sterling qualities had there gained for him the honest liking of his neighbors. He was now nearly sixty years old, lean and rugged, with a physique like iron and limbs that never tired. He was a master of woodcraft, as many a wary Indian had learned, and his aim rarely missed. With the fearlessness of a lion and the stealth of a panther, he combined the vision of a hawk and the hearing of a deer. Altogether, he was such a friend as Nathan might well count worth having.

Many of the Wyoming men were weak and exhausted, and though the march was kept up at a fairly good speed, it was not fast enough to suit Barnabas. So, at noon of the third day, July 1st, when the party had halted for a brief

rest in the lonely country, miles to the northwest
of Trenton, the old woodsman suggested that himself and half a dozen others—naming those most
capable of speed and endurance—should push on
in advance of the main band. He urged as a reason the necessity for letting their imperiled
friends know that aid was on the way, so that
they might hold out with better spirit. The
possession of Captain Stanbury's papers was
purely a minor reason with Barnabas, as he
frankly admitted to Nathan. "The first object
of the journey is to save the settlements, lad,"
he said; "but of course we'll dig up these
papers as soon as we git a chance."

The officers commanding the troops promptly
recognized the wisdom of the suggested course.
Barnabas chose Nathan — whose wind and
strength well fitted him for the purpose—and
five brave and hardy men of his own company.
They started at once, taking plenty of ammunition and supplies for three days, and were a mile
on their way when the main body which they
left behind, began the afternoon's march.

The region stretching northwest to the Susquehanna at Wilkesbarre was wild and lonely, but Barnabas knew every foot of the way. He avoided the circuitous bridle-road, and led the party by narrow and direct trails of his own choosing — over rugged and dismal mountain passes, through forests where deer and bear, turkeys and pheasants abounded, and across streams that teemed with fish.

By the aid of an early moon they traveled until ten o'clock that night, and after sleeping soundly in the woods, and without camp-fires, they resumed their march at daybreak. About the middle of the morning, coming to an open glade by a spring, they made a startling discovery. Here a party of horsemen had plainly spent the previous night. The ground was trodden by hoofs and footmarks. The ashes of two fires were still warm, and close by were heaps of pine-boughs that had served for bedding.

"Who can they have been?" asked Nathan.

"I can't guess, lad," replied Barnabas, shaking his head, "an' it's hard to say where they're bound for. They ain't been gone long, an' from the looks of things they numbered nine or ten. We must have crossed their trail somewhere's back without seein' it. From here," stepping forward and pointing to the trodden grass, "they went almost due north. I reckon they're striking for the bridle-road yonder, which runs sort of parallel with the course we're making—"

He stopped suddenly as he spied a glittering object at his feet: "A Britisher's spur!" he exclaimed, picking it up. "An' the pattern the dragoons wear. What on earth does this mean?"

"It means a squad of the enemy's cavalry, Barnabas," declared Evan Jones.

"I believe you, man," said Barnabas, "who else but the cussed British would have cut limbs for bedding? An' the camp-fires show that they didn't reckon on any other travelers bein' in the neighborhood. I'm clean beat to know—"

"Here's something else," interrupted Nathan, handing Barnabas a large horn button of an odd color.

"The old man looked at it intently. His

eyes flashed, and his teeth showed behind his parted lips. "Simon Glass!" he cried.

"Simon Glass?" echoed three or four voices.

"Aye, Simon Glass, men," repeated Barnabas. "I'll swear to this button. It came off his buckskin coat, an' the inhuman fiend lost it here hisself."

"I've heard of Simon Glass," Nathan said curiously. "Who is he?"

"You don't want to meet him, lad," Barnabas answered grimly. "If ever there was a devil in human shape he's that same. He's a little squatty man, with one eye out; but the other's worth half a dozen. An' his face is a criss-cross of knife-scars.

"There ain't any crime too bad for the wretch," Barnabas continued earnestly. "Until eight years back he lived about Wyoming, an' every one was afraid of him. He shot two men what crossed him, an' robbed an' murdered another. Then he had to light out, an' the next heard of him was that he'd killed a man an' woman up at Niagara. When the war

9

begun he turned Tory an' joined the British, an' since then they say he's killed a heap of Americans in cold blood. I have a score agin him, an' I won't forget it. An' as for this old buckskin coat—why, he's been wearin' it steady for fifteen years, an' he wore it on this very spot last night. I know the buttons."

"What can he be doing here?" asked a Scotchman named Collum McNicol.

"He may have some bloody work of his own on hand," replied Barnabas, "but it's more likely he's been hired to lead these dragoons up to join Butler's forces at Wyoming. An' yet it ain't natural for such a little handful of British to march a hundred and fifty miles up country from Clinton's army. Well, it's no use guessin'. We can't overtake the party, seein' they're mounted, and p'raps it's just as well. But if we do run across 'em—along the way or up at Wyoming, I'll have a bullet ready for Simon Glass. We've fooled too long, men—march on."

Rapidly, and with untiring speed, the little band of seven filed on through the forest paths, while the sun crept from horizon to horizon. Barnabas was in a sober and thoughtful mood, and his companions could not shake off a feeling of impending ill. Brave men though they were, the presence of Simon Glass in the vicinity was enough to unsteady their nerves. Eyes were keen and ears alert as they advanced.

About the middle of the afternoon footsteps were heard in front, and down dropped every man to cover. Seven musket barrels were in line with the stranger as he came in sight among the trees—a bearded settler in gray homespun.

"Hooray! Luke Shippen!" cried Barnabas, jumping up, and soon the whole party were shaking hands with an old friend and neighbor.

"Where's the rest of the troops?" was the new-comer's first question. "I've come to hurry them up."

"Are they needed sorely?" asked Barnabas.

"Aye, men," Shippen replied. "When I left Wilkesbarre night afore last Colonel John Butler was up above the valley at the mouth of the Lackawanna, with a force of Tories and Indians from Canada. He's holding off for reinforce-ments, but they may come any time. Our peo-ple are in the forts, but they won't be able to offer much resistance."

"God help them!" muttered Barnabas. "Push on, Luke. You'll find the Wyoming troops half a day's march behind. Bid them travel with all haste. Meanwhile, we'll let no grass grow under our feet."

"I'll trust you for that, man. I'm off."

"Wait," added Barnabas. "You met none on the way, Luke?"

"Not a soul. Why do you ask?"

"No matter," said Barnabas. "Good-bye."

"Good-bye, comrade," replied Shippen, and his long strides quickly carried him out of sight.

"Now for a hard march," said Barnabas to his men, "and God grant we arrive in time. We are sorely needed, few as we are."

Twilight came, and a brief interval of dark-ness, and then the glow of the rising moon. For mile after mile the little band pressed on, heed-

less of hunger and weariness, and it was close
to midnight when their leader halted them on a
far-stretching plateau high up among the mountains, sparsely timbered with pine and oak.

" Here we'll spend what little of the night is
left, bein' as we're all done out," declared Barnabas. " I know the spot. Wyoming is but
six or eight miles off, an' we'll make it afore to-
morrow noon. Now for supper an' rest."

Rations were served out and eaten, and then
Barnabas divided the night into three watches
and assigned the men to duty. Reuben Atwood's turn came first, and the soft step of the
sentry was the last sound the weary men heard
as they fell asleep on the fragrant pine needles.

Nathan slumbered for hours, too fatigued
even to dream, and then he suddenly opened his
eyes and sat up, barely able to repress a cry. A
small snake glided from his side, and he knew
that the cold touch of the reptile on his hand
had wakened him.

His companions were sleeping around him,
but he saw nothing of the sentry. Looking

further his eyes rested on an open glade, bathed in moonlight, that was twenty feet away among the trees. Cold perspiration started on his brow, and he trembled from head to foot. His breath came quick and hard. Was it a real or a ghostly visitant—that slim figure standing in the centre of the glade; that familiar face staring toward him, with its every feature clear in the moon's silver glow?

CHAPTER VIII

IN WHICH SIMON GLASS MAKES A VERY STRANGE REMARK

LITTLE wonder that the lad shivered; that cold sweat started on cheeks and brow; that, at first, he knew not whether he was awake or dreaming! For the face in the moonlight was Godfrey Spencer's, and so were the step and figure as the intruder crept stealthily nearer.

The camp was in deep shadow, and Nathan himself could not be seen. For a few seconds he watched and trembled in mute horror, unable to utter a sound. "I am not asleep," he decided, feeling the night breeze on his hot temples. "Am I going mad? That can't be Godfrey. Yes, it is—"

Just then the spell was broken by the snap of a dry twig under the supposed Godfrey's tread. He slipped to one side of the glade, showing a short, thick-set man behind him, and both darted back into the shadow as Nathan sprang up with a cry that echoed far through the forest. At the same instant the missing sentry scrambled to his feet from the left of the camp, where he had fallen asleep, and down he went again, almost as quickly, as a musket-shot rang out of the darkness. Barnabas and his companions, now fully roused, ran this way and that in confusion, inquiring the cause of the alarm. "They're gone now," exclaimed Nathan, and he briefly told what he had seen.

There was a rush to the spot where the sentry had fallen. Robert Lindsay, who had taken the second watch, lay dead with a bullet through his heart. A clay pipe, long since cold, was still clutched between his teeth, and near by a little patch of dry grass and pine-needles was burnt close to the ground. A shuddering fear fell on the men as they looked at the body of their comrade and fierce were the threats of vengeance.

"It's plain as daylight what happened," said the keen-witted Barnabas. "The British have a camp over yonder by the bridle-road," pointing northward. "They traveled slow yesterday, an' we just about caught up with 'em at midnight. Then poor Lindsay here lights his pipe for a smoke, and sets fire to the grass. Before he kin outen it the enemy see the blaze an' come creepin' over. By that time Lindsay had fell asleep, an' small blame to him arter the march we made."

"He was sort of drowsy when I roused him for his turn," said Atwood. "I wish I'd let him sleep."

"He's sleepin' now," Abel Cutbush answered, softly, "and I reckon right here will have to be his grave for the present. We couldn't bury him in this hard ground, even if we had the tools."

"Or the time," said Barnabas, "which we can't spare. He was a brave soldier an' a true friend, an' I say it who knows. God rest his soul!"

"We'd better be seeking his murderer," grumbled Collum McNicol, and the rest approved warmly.

"Have a bit of patience, men," replied Barnabas. "It's no use to pursue now." Turning to Nathan he added: "The little man was surely Simon Glass, lad. Are you certain about the other?"

"The one in front was Godfrey Spencer," declared Nathan.

"The fellow who looks summat like you?" asked Barnabas. "I seen him at De Vries's house two years ago, when I brought a letter from your father."

"Yes," replied Nathan. "He's a lieutenant in the British army now, and I believe he is attached to Major Langdon's staff."

"Major Langdon?" exclaimed Barnabas. "That's the name of the prisoner I lost! I wonder if he is with the party."

"Very likely, since Godfrey is here," Nathan suggested.

Barnabas scratched his head thoughtfully for a moment, seeing in this affair a relation to certain other things that had puzzled him considerably of late.

"I'm forgetting my duty," he said. "It ain't safe to stay here a minute longer. Forward, now, an' make no noise."

With loaded muskets, the men fell in behind their leader, leaving the body of poor Lindsay to stiffen on the grass. Barnabas led the party about a hundred yards to the northeast and halted them in a cluster of pine trees.

"You're safe from attack here," he said. "Don't stir till I come back. I'm going forward a bit to reconnoiter."

Several volunteered for this duty, but Barnabas knew that he was best fitted for it, and he had his way. He crept off as noiselessly as a serpent, and the shadows hid him from view.

Nathan and his companions waited anxiously in the dark cover, not daring to speak above a whisper, and expecting at any moment to hear a shot. Fully half an hour elapsed, and dawn was beginning to break when Barnabas returned.

"I've been to the enemy's camp," he announced, eagerly. "They're less than a mile due north from here, across a creek that flows

through a deep an' narrow ravine.   An' just on
the other side of the creek an' the camp is the
bridle-road.   There's a big pine tree fell across
the chasm, formin' a natural bridge from bank
to bank, an' I crept over that to peek an' listen."

"Are they going to attack us?" asked Reuben
Atwood.

"They're thinkin' more of gettin' away," replied Barnabas.   "From what I kin make out
they're in a hurry to reach Wyoming, an' they
propose to start as soon as they've had breakfast.
They're at the cookin' now, just as though we
wasn't in the neighborhood to be reckoned with.
The spies didn't learn our strength a bit ago,
an' that's why they're doubtful about attackin'."

"Is Major Langdon there?" inquired Nathan.

"No, lad, he ain't; but unless my ears deceived me, it was him give the party their orders.
I seen young Godfrey Spencer sittin' by the
fire.   An' Simon Glass was there, as big as life,
waitin' for the bullet that's in my pouch to reach
his black heart.   There's nine in the party—all
British cavalrymen, except Glass—but they're

wearin' plain clothes instead of uniforms. The horses are the same way—no brass nor polished leather fixin's."

" I reckon they want to pass for Americans," said Evan Jones.

"That's just it," assented Barnabas. "An' now look to your flints, men, an' your powder an' ball. I'm going to lead you straight agin' the enemy. We'll shin over the tree, and fall on 'em by surprise. If they expect us at all, they're countin' on our comin' round to the bridle-road by the ford, which is five hundred yards further up the creek."

" We're six to nine, Barnabas," McNicol suggested in a dubious tone.

" We're worth a dozen Britishers, man," stoutly declared Barnabas. " We'll have the first fire, an' that ought to drop five or six of the enemy. The rest will run—if I knows 'em right—and then we'll grab the horses. It's the horses we want most. They'll take us gallopin' over the bridle-road, and into Wyoming early in the morning."

Barnabas had struck the right chord. The hope of reaching their imperiled families within a few hours was a stronger inducement to the men than vengeance for poor Lindsay. Without a dissenting voice they approved their leader's plan, and examined their loadings and flints. Five minutes later they were following Barnabas in single file through the thick wood, now cold and gray in the breaking light of dawn.

Nathan alone was gloomy and sad. At every step he saw before his eyes a mental picture that made him shudder. "Godfrey will be there," he reflected. "He may kill me, or I may have to fire at him. Somebody else will likely shoot him if I don't. He is a Tory and an enemy, and he betrayed me that night in Philadelphia; but I can't forget that we were old friends. I must do my duty, though. And I will do it, come what may."

He compressed his lips, and marched on resolutely.

With a warning gesture Barnabas halted; and the men behind him, half hidden in the laurel scrub, shifted their muskets noiselessly, and peered past their leader with strained, intent faces.

There was danger in the still air. Tragedy and death brooded over this dense woody spot in the mountainous solitudes of Pennsylvania. The brink of the chasm was three yards away —a chasm that dropped seventy feet, between narrow, hollowed-out walls of rock, to the deep and sluggish waters of the creek. Through the vistas of foliage and timber could be seen the trunk of the fallen pine, with many a bushy offshoot, that spanned the gorge from bank to bank. But there was no sound of enemy's voices on the farther side; no evidence of the camp save a curl of gray smoke drifting upward to the blue sky, now rosy-flushed with the first light of day.

"Looks like they'd finished their breakfast an' gone," Barnabas said, in a low voice; "but then, ag'in, they may be layin' a trap fur us. It ain't safe ter calkerlate when Simon Glass is around."

"We'll do no good tarrying here, man," grumbled McNicol. "Yonder's the tree, and we're ready to follow."

Barnabas thought of poor Lindsay and then of the horses, and suddenly flung prudence to the winds. "Forward!" he whispered, and starting quickly through the scrub he planted his feet on the fallen pine. Nathan followed with a beating heart, and the next man had just stepped out when a musket-barrel was poked from the bushes across the chasm.

"Back, men," roared Barnabas. "Get to cover," and as he turned around and gained the rear bank by an agile spring, a thunderous report woke the echoes of the gorge.

Nathan tried to leap also, but it was too late. He saw the flash and the puff and felt a stinging pain on the right side of his head. All grew dark before him. He tottered, lost his balance, and fell. His hands, clutching at the empty air, caught a projecting limb, and he held to it with desperate strength. As he hung dangling over the gulf, dizzy and stupefied, he heard a harsh voice above cry out: "You fired too soon, you fool. Let the rebels have it now, men. Blaze away at the bushes."

A straggling discharge of musketry followed the words, and then Nathan's fingers slipped. He shot downward forty feet to the bushy top of a tree that grew slantwise from the wall of the gorge. This broke the violence of his fall, but it did not stop him. He bounded from branch to branch, and fell the remaining distance to the creek, plunging head first beneath the surface.

The instinct of life was strong within the lad, and his struggles soon brought him to the surface, choking and gasping. He was too bruised and stunned to swim a fair stroke, but by feeble paddling he managed to keep his head above water.

That was all he thought about in his dazed condition, and without making an attempt to reach either shore he drifted with the sluggish current for twenty yards or so. Then he saw a conical rock close ahead, rising several feet out

10

of mid-stream, and by an effort he reached it and clasped both arms around the top.

There he clung for fully five minutes, while strength returned and his mind cleared. He had not heard a sound since he fell, and he wondered if all his companions were dead. He listened in vain, looking up at the distant blue vault of the sky. The silence of death rested on wood and stream.

A sharp pain suddenly recalled the fact that he had been shot, and he put one hand to his head in a fever of apprehension. His fingers were red with blood when he looked at them, but his fear was gone. The bullet had merely grazed his brow, leaving a narrow skin wound.

This discovery put new life into Nathan, and he determined to get to shore and search for his friends, if they were still alive. But as he was about to let go of the rock he heard a noise from the north bank, in which direction he was facing. Here the slope was less precipitous than above, and was heavily timbered.

Some person was descending toward the

stream at a recklessly rapid speed. Loosened stones rolled down to the water with a splash. Here and there amid the trees and bushes a dark form showed at intervals. Was it friend or foe? Nathan asked himself, and all too soon the question was answered.

The noise suddenly ceased, and from out the fringe of laurel at the base of the slope peered a man's face—a hideous countenance with but one eye, and with skin like wrinkled parchment slashed by a quillful of purple ink. It needed not a glimpse of a dingy buckskin jacket with horn buttons to tell Nathan that this was the terrible Simon Glass.

The face was followed by a long-barrelled musket, but the ruffian did not at once raise it to his shoulder. He stared keenly at the lad for a moment, and then grinned like a fiend.

"No mistake about it, that's him," he muttered aloud. "Die, you dirty rebel," he added, levelling the gun and squinting along the tube with his one eye.

Nathan heard the first words so indistinctly that they caused him no wonder, but the sentence that followed chilled his very blood. He could neither move nor utter a sound as he faced the death that seemed certain. A spell was upon him. He was charmed into helplessness by the musket's black mouth—by the ghastly grin on the one-eyed Tory's face.

A few seconds slipped by, and they were like so many minutes to the tortured lad. Then, just as Glass pressed the trigger, a fusillade of musketry rang out from some point up the bluff. Bang! went the Tory's gun, but the surprise of the shooting overhead had fortunately spoilt his aim. The bullet hit the rock within two inches of Nathan's face, and a shower of splintered chips flew around him.

Crack! — crack! — crack! —crack! — crack! The muskets were blazing merrily, and there was a din of yells and cheers. Nathan looked up, and saw two figures dart across the pine-tree bridge. A third had gained the centre when a bullet sent him plunging down to the creek.

The lad let go of the rock, dived, and came to the surface. Over on the bank Simon Glass was reloading. He had driven the powder in, when the firing suddenly ceased, and now he seemed to hesitate.

"Help! help!" Nathan yelled loudly. There was an answering shout from the summit of the gorge, and then a crashing noise. The Tory glanced above him, tossed his partly loaded musket over his shoulder, and ran swiftly down the edge of the stream. He was soon hidden from sight in the bushes.

"That you, Nathan?" called a familiar voice. Nathan answered lustily, and a dozen strokes brought him to shore just as Barnabas Otter reached the foot of the bluff.

"Thank God! lad," cried the old man. "I gave you up for dead when you fell off the tree."

When Nathan had told his story, Barnabas declared that it would be both useless and perilous to pursue Simon Glass. "We'll settle with the ruffian another time," he said. "To think of his creepin' down here to make sure you was dead! But that's jist like him. An' now, if you're able, we'll be gettin' back to the party."

Nathan was all right except for a slight weakness, and with a little assistance he made fair progress up the bank. As they climbed, Barnabas told what had happened. "We got under cover too quick for the enemy," he explained, "an' while they thought we was hiding in the wood we were making for the ford on a trot. It was round a bend of the creek, and luckily we got across without bein' seen. Then we circled around to the camp, and surprised the British from the rear as they were getting to saddle. We dropped three in their tracks, an' shot another on the bridge, an' the rest cut an' run fur life. It's a pity Simon Glass wasn't there then."

"Any of our men killed?" asked Nathan.

"Evan Jones," Barnabas answered, soberly. "He was shot by a little chap that fired as he run."

By this time they were at the captured camp, and Nathan was warmly greeted. He examined the four dead dragoons, but Godfrey was not among them.

"What did the man look like who was shot on the tree?" he asked.

"He was my age, and had a heavy mustache," replied Reuben Atwood; and the lad's mind was relieved.

It was considered expedient to start while the five survivors of the enemy were scattered, and before they could get together. Three horses had been killed in the assault—they being in direct range—and a fourth was so badly crippled as to be useless. The five that remained were just enough for the party, now reduced by two.

While the men gathered up what muskets, ammunition, and other stuff had fallen into their hands, Barnabas dressed Nathan's skin-wound and squeezed his clothes partly dry. Once in the saddle the lad felt quite himself again, though he shuddered frequently to think of his narrow escape.

The victory was not without its sting. Poor

Lindsay and Jones had answered their last summons, and the bodies had to be left where they had fallen. Their comrades would gladly have buried them, but duty to the imperiled settlers at Wyoming forbade a moment's delay.

The sun was just peeping above the horizon when the little band mounted the captured horses and rode away from the scene of death and bloodshed. For the first two miles they kept close watch as they trotted along the bridle-road, and then, the chance of a surprise being now past, they urged their steeds to a gallop.

But the country was very rugged, and the road winding, and it was necessary to walk or trot the horses much of the way. So it was close to nine o'clock of the morning when the travelers rode out on the elevated crest of the mountainous plateau, and beheld the lovely Wyoming Valley spread out before them in the soft July sunlight.

Here was the Susquehanna winding in a silver loop from mountain gap to mountain gap.

There, a little to the westward, the hamlet of Wilkesbarre nestled at the base of the hills. Farther east the stockade of Forty Fort rose from the opposite lying bank of the river, and the flag was still fluttering from its staff.

CHAPTER IX

IN WHICH NATHAN TAKES PART IN THE BATTLE OF WYOMING

Barnabas and his companions checked their horses, and for several minutes they sat still in the saddle, gazing with stirring emotions on the peaceful and beautiful scene. In vain they listened for hostile shots; in vain they scanned the horizon for the smoke and flames of burning dwellings.

"We've come in time!" exclaimed Nathan.

"We have, lad; no doubt of it," assented Barnabas. "God grant the rest of the force get here before the trouble begins. And now let's be pushing down to the fort."

"Hold on, comrades," said Abel Cutbush. "Here our ways must separate. I'm a married man, and I'm going to strike fur Wilkesbarre, where my wife and child will be expecting me."

154

"They may be yonder at the fort," suggested Barnabas.

"Perhaps, man," was the reply; "but I'll look at home first."

So, with a few words of farewell, Cutbush turned sharply off to the left. The other four urged their steeds cautiously down the mountain-side, and without mishap they reached the valley. They crossed the Susquehanna by a fording, spurred up the farther bank, and were shortly challenged by watchful sentries. A little later they rode triumphantly through the gates of Forty Fort, which was a large, stockaded inclosure with double rows of huts inside.

Here thrilling sights were to be seen, and it was evident that a battle or a siege was shortly expected. The fort was full of men, women, and children. The former were hard at work, cleaning and loading muskets, measuring out powder and ball, and repairing clothes and shoes for a march. Many of these eager defenders ranged in age from fourteen to sixteen, and there were also a number of very old men. The little children were prattling and playing as though they had been brought to the fort for a holiday. Of the women, some had given way to utter grief and were weeping bitterly ; others, more stout of heart, were cheering and encouraging their husbands.

Barnabas and his companions were joyfully greeted, many friends and relatives pressing around to clasp their hands. When the first excitement was over Colonel Zebulon Butler pushed to the spot, accompanied by his associate officers, Colonels Denison and Dorrance.

" My brave fellows, you are heartily welcome," cried Colonel Butler. " Do you come from Washington ? What news do you bring ? Where are the rest of the Wyoming men ?"

"A couple of days' march behind, sir," replied Barnabas, in answer to the latter question. Then he briefly went on to tell of the battle of Monmouth, the departure of the Wyoming troops, and the subsequent adventures of his own little party. Men and women listened to the narrative with breathless attention, and when they learned of the uncertain fate of Captain Stanbury—who was known and liked throughout the valley—Nathan was the recipient of numerous looks and words of sympathy. But all other news dwindled to insignificance beside the fact that the relieving force was still miles away, and how sorely the absent ones were needed Barnabas and his friends soon understood.

It appeared, according to Colonel Butler's hasty account, that the enemy had entered the head of the valley on the 30th of June. They numbered more than a thousand in all, six or seven hundred of them being bloodthirsty Seneca Indians under the terrible half-breed Brandt, and the remainder consisting of Colonel John Butler's Rangers, Captain Caldwell's Royal Greens, and Tories from Pennsylvania, New Jersey, and New York. Colonel John Butler, who was in no wise related to the patriot leader, was in full command.

The enemy were too strong in numbers to be successfully resisted, and since the first of July they had ruthlessly murdered half a score of settlers, taken possession of Fort Jenkins, the uppermost one in the valley, and had advanced to the next fort, called Wintermoot's. Here they now were, on this morning of the 3d of July, and it was believed that they were preparing to move on Forty Fort.

"So you see that the situation is critical," Colonel Butler concluded. "We have not yet decided what to do, but the day can hardly pass without action of some sort. It is useless to hope for aid from the relieving force—they cannot arrive in time. The little army assembled here now under my command, is all we can count upon. They have come mostly from the neighboring lower part of the valley. A few companies of our home regiment are unfortunately in the outer settlements, and they can't reach us inside of twenty-four hours."

"Then we must get along without them, sir," exclaimed Barnabas. "We'll give the Tories such a lesson as Washington gave Clinton at Monmouth a few days ago."

"God grant that we may!" Colonel Butler said fervently. "I expect word shortly concerning the movements of the enemy, and then will be the time to form our plans. And now, my good men, I want to thank you for your heroic march. You will be provided with food, and everything else you may need, and I shall depend on your support in the coming struggle."

"You are sure to have it, sir," declared Barnabas; and this opinion was eagerly echoed by the rest.

During the next hour the work of preparation went on, fresh recruits straggling in at intervals. Nathan and his companions, who were already fully equipped, lent what aid they could, or engaged in conversation with old friends and neighbors.

About eleven o'clock in the morning a settler named Ingersoll, who had been captured by the enemy several days before, near Wintermoot's fort, arrived under a flag of truce, in custody of an Indian and a Tory. He was the bearer of a message from Colonel John Butler, demanding the immediate and unconditional surrender of all the forts in the valley and all public property. This was, of course, refused, and Ingersoll left with his guards, the latter having taken advantage of their visit to observe the condition of the fort, and the number and spirit of its defenders.

Colonel Zebulon Butler now called a council of war, at which opinions were freely expressed. Many of the settlers were admitted to this, including Barnabas and his companions. Colonels Denison and Dorrance, as well as a number of others, were in favor of delaying action, on the ground that the absent militia companies and the relief force sent by Washington might yet arrive in time to save the valley. But Colonel Butler was opposed to delay, and made an eloquent oration against it.

"For three days the enemy have been within the valley," he said, "and they have steadily carried on their work of destruction and murder. Two forts are already in their possession, and if we show an inclination to be idle they will certainly press their advantage. They have boats, and they can easily cross the river from Wintermoot's to Pittston, and take the little fort there under Captain Blanchard. They can march or float from place to place, and will destroy the valley piecemeal. And once the butchers spread throughout the country, we will no longer be able to hold our little army together. Each man will fly to protect his own home. The relief force cannot reach us in time, and it is doubtful if the absent militia companies will arrive within two days. So we must clearly depend on God and ourselves, and I assert that to attack and defeat the enemy is the only hope for the settlement."

These spirited words made an impression, and at once won over a large majority. The rest were finally induced to assent, and without further delay the preparations for the advance were begun.

Six companies were available, and of these one consisted of regulars under Captain Hewitt.

11

The others were as follows: Captain Whittlesey's company, from Plymouth; Captain McKarrican's, from Hanover; the Lower Wilkesbarre and Upper Wilkesbarre Companies, commanded respectively by Captain Bidlack and Captain Geer, and a company from Kingston under Captain Aholiab Buck. Barnabas and Nathan were assigned to Captain Whittlesey's company, as were also Reuben Atwood and Collum McNicol. In all, the force was three hundred strong—two hundred and thirty enrolled men, and about seventy boys, elderly settlers, judges of the valley courts, and civil magistrates. And this brave but meager army was about to attack one thousand Tories and Indians!

It was an hour past noon when the band of defenders filed out through the gates of Forty Fort, leaving a few sentries behind them to protect the weeping and well-nigh distracted women and children. It was a clear, warm day, and never had the Wyoming Valley looked more beautiful and peaceful. Birds were twittering, and the sun shone brightly on forest and river.

Forward the column marched, not knowing that their movements were being watched by vigilant spies. But such was the case, and fleet couriers bore word of the advance to Colonel . John Butler, at Wintermoot's. He at once sent a message to his rear guard at Fort Jenkins, who were destroying the defenses of that place, to hasten down to join him and meet the Yankees.

In the neighborhood of three o'clock the Americans approached Wintermoot's fort, and from a distance they saw that it was in flames— the motive for which act on the enemy's part was never fully understood. At this point there were two plains between the river and the mountain, the upper and lower flats being divided by a steep bank fifteen or twenty feet in height. The fort stood on the brow of the bluff.

Colonel Zebulon Butler sent several officers forward to reconnoiter the ground, and when they returned with their reports, and with the intelligence that the foe were close in front, the little army at once proceeded to form in line of battle. They ascended the dividing bluff, and deployed across the upper plain. Their right rested on the steep bank, and the left stretched across the flat to a morass that separated the bottom land from the mountain. The plain was sparsely wooded with yellow pine trees and oak scrubs. Captain Whittlesey's company, to which Nathan and his friends belonged, was on the extreme left, and that flank was in charge of Colonels Denison and Dorrance. Colonel Butler himself commanded the right wing.

The enemy's left, under Colonel John Butler, rested on Wintermoot's fort, which was now on fire, and from which the Susquehanna was distant about eighty rods. A flanking party of Indian marksmen were hidden in some logs and bushes near the top of the bank. Next to Colonel John Butler were more Indian marksmen and Caldwell's Royal Greens, while the main body of the Senecas under Brandt formed the right wing, which extended over the plain to the morass.

Thus face to face, the two armies remained inactive for some little time. At a distance Nathan's keen eyes could make out the glitter of a uniform here and there, or see the feathered plumes of the Indians nodding. Through the green of the trees the sun shone on tomahawks and musket barrels.

"How do you feel, lad?" asked old Barnabas.

"Ready for the fight," was the cool reply.

"But this ain't the battle of Monmouth, lad. There's worse odds ag'in us."

"All the more reason why we should fight the better," declared Nathan. "Monmouth was for our country and this is for our homes."

"Ay, that's proper talk," exclaimed Reuben Atwood. "I'm thinkin' we must all fight to the bitter end, since there's no mercy to be looked for from them fiends over yonder."

Now a sudden excitement spread throughout the lines, and the men straightened up at attention. Colonel Zebulon Butler came riding from right to left, and checking his horse near Captain Whittlesey's company he repeated the brief address he had just made to his followers on the right.

"Men, we are about to attack," he cried. "Yonder is the enemy. Slaughter without mercy is what we must expect if we are defeated. We are here to fight for liberty, for our homes and families, for life itself. Stand firm with the first shock, and the Indians will yield. Let every man remember his duty."

Loud and hearty cheers followed the Colonel as he rode back to his post. Nathan gripped his musket tight, and as he recalled the massacres of the preceding days he resolved to make each shot tell. "Hurrah! we're going!" he shouted.

"Yes, we're at it, lad," cried Barnabas. "Steady, now!"

The signal had been given, and the long line was in forward motion. They drew nearer and nearer, and suddenly the order to fire came from Colonel Zebulon Butler. Crash! crash!

the deadly volleys rang out. Still the Americans advanced, firing rapidly and steadily. Crash! Crash! Men began to fall, some dead and some wounded. The bluish powder smoke rolled over the field, mingling with the yellow clouds from the burning fort. Louder and louder blazed the musketry fire. In spite of the pluck of its officers the British line gave way a little. But it quickly rallied, and the enemy stood their ground stubbornly.

The American right was now hotly engaged with the Senecas and Rangers, and soon the fight was waging along the entire line. On both sides the dead and wounded increased, and as the Indian sharpshooters fired they uttered fearful and hideous yells. Nathan was surprised at his own coolness. He loaded and fired like an old soldier, never pulling trigger until he had a bead drawn on a foe. Some of the men on the left began to waver as their comrades fell about them, but a few words from Colonel Dorrance had the effect of closing the broken line up.

For half an hour the battle went on, growing warmer and warmer. As yet Nathan was unhurt, and so far as he could tell his friends had fared as fortunately. Animated by the hope of victory, the Americans displayed the utmost valor and bravery. But now, alas! the enemy began to show the power that superior numbers gave them. A large force of Indians was thrown into the swamp, thus completely outflanking the left of the patriot line. Seeing the danger, Colonel Denison ordered Whittlesey to wheel his company at an angle with the main line, and thus present a front to the foe.

It is always difficult to perform such an evolution under a hot fire, and in this case the result was disastrous. No sooner had Captain Whittlesey's company made the attempt than the Indians rushed forward with blood-curdling yells. Some of the Americans understood the order to fall back on flank to mean a retreat, and by this fatal mistake the whole of the left line was thrown into confusion. A part stood their ground, and others fled in panic. Seeing the disorder and confusion here, and finding that his own men on the right were also beginning to give way, Colonel Zebulon Butler rode recklessly to and fro between the fires of the opposing ranks.

"Stand firm!" he cried in ringing tones. "Don't forsake me! Make a stand, my brave men, and the victory will yet be ours."

But it was too late. In vain did the daring commander harangue his men; in vain did his officers support him by words and actions, and the drummers beat the charge. The rout began —a rout that was too overwhelming and widespread to be checked. The right and left lines of the Americans fled in all directions, hotly pursued by the vengeful Tories and Indians. The crack of muskets and the dull crash of the tomahawk mingled with the shrieks of the dying and the yells of the victors. Stephen Whiton, a young schoolmaster, was butchered by the side of the man whose daughter he had just married. Darius Spofford, also lately married, fell dead in the arms of his brother Phineas. Every captain that led a company into action was slain. Bidlack, Hewitt, Whittlesey —all died at the head of their men.

And now, the battle over and the massacre begun, horror was piled on horror. There was little chance of escape for the fugitives. The flanking party of Indians pushed hastily to the rear to cut off the retreat to Forty Fort, and thus the wretched and panic-stricken settlers were driven in the direction of the river, over the open ground and through fields of uncut grain. Some few swam to Monockasy Island, which offered a temporary refuge. But many were speared and tomahawked at the water's edge, and others, shot while swimming, were borne away lifeless on the current. A man named Pensil, who had gained the island, was pursued there and slain by his own Tory brother. Lieutenant Shoemaker, as he plunged into the river, glanced over his shoulder to see a Tory named Windecker who had often dined at his table in past times. Swimming back to shore, he begged his old friend to protect him. The foul ruffian pretended to consent, but while he helped the officer out of the water with his left hand, with his right he drove a tomahawk into his brain. Many others were thus lured to shore by promise of quarter, only to be ruthlessly butchered. A number of the prisoners were thrown alive on the burning logs of Fort Wintermoot, and no less than a score were tomahawked by Queen Esther, an Indian fury in the form of a woman. She slew them with her own hand while the savages held them, and the bodies of her victims, scalped and mutilated, were subsequently found lying in a circle where they had fallen. The carnage would have been greater had not night intervened. Under cover of darkness a small proportion of the fugitives escaped, and of the number was Colonel Denison and Colonel Zebulon Butler. The latter was borne off the field on his horse, and by a devious route he finally reached the fort at Wilkesbarre.

Good fortune also fell to the lot of Barnabas and Nathan. After standing their ground until valor had ceased to be a virtue they fled, side by side, to the river, firing at intervals as they went. At the water's edge they confronted and killed a Tory and an Indian who had overtaken them, and then, being good swimmers, they safely reached the opposite shore some distance below the island. In company with several other refugees they pushed down the Susquehanna, recrossed the stream, and safely entered Forty Fort at nightfall. They were rejoiced to learn that Reuben Atwood and Collum McNicol had arrived some time before.

Pitiful and heartrending were the scenes within the fort as the hours of darkness dragged on. Women and children wept and wrung their hands as they called the names of loved ones who would never return. Bleeding and powder-grimed men stood about in weary and dazed groups. Of the band of three hundred who started out to battle at noon-time less than one-third had straggled back. The rest lay dead and mutilated in the woods, on the sands of Monockasy Island, or were drifting on the rippling tide of the river. So terrible was the defeat that the survivors had utterly lost heart; they were ready to submit to any terms to save their lives.

The night was full of horror, for an attack was constantly expected. In the interval between darkness and dawn, a few settlers with their families flocked to the fort from the lower part of the valley, and several sorely-wounded fugitives crept in. Nathan could not sleep, and for hours he wandered about the stockade. The disaster had stunned him, unused as he was to the horrors of Indian warfare. The past week, with its record of bloodshed and battle, had made a man of the lad. How dreamlike and long ago seemed his happy student life in Philadelphia!

The outcome of the Tory and Indian raid upon the colonists of the Wyoming Valley may be briefly told. On the morning of the 4th of July—the day following the massacre—Colonel Zebulon Butler started for the nearest town on the Lehigh to send a report to the Board of War. That morning one of the absent militia companies arrived at Forty Fort, and there was some talk of offering further resistance. But this was speedily abandoned, as messengers who had been sent out reported that the panic-stricken inhabitants of the valley were fleeing in every direction to the wilderness. It was also learned that Fort Brown, at Pittston, had been surrendered by Captain Blanchard.

So Colonel Denison at once opened negotiations with the leaders of the enemy, and after hours of suspense and discussion it was decided to surrender the fort on condition that the lives of the survivors should be spared. The articles of capitulation were signed, and on the afternoon of the 5th a sad and bitter ceremony took place on the bluff of the Susquehanna. The gates of Forty Fort were thrown open, the flag was hauled down, and to the music of drums and fifes the enemy marched in behind Colonel John Butler—company after company of Rangers and Tories, Captain Caldwell's Royal Greens, and the sullen, painted-faced Indians headed by two human fiends—Brandt and Queen Esther.

Colonel Butler prevented any immediate bloodshed, but the settlers were ruthlessly plundered as they filed out. Knowing their danger too well they fled in all directions, some toward the Delaware, others down the Susquehanna by water and land.

The Senecas and Tories shortly laid waste the valley, destroying what they could not take away, burning the town of Wilkesbarre and many cabins, and driving the horses and cattle to Niagara. The relief force that had started from Washington's army turned back when the news of the massacre reached them at Stroudsburg, and for a time the lovely Vale of Wyoming was abandoned to ruin and solitude.

CHAPTER X

AMONG the last to leave Forty Fort after its surrender was Barnabas Otter. In the dusk of the evening he slipped through the gate with others, and made his way, unobserved, to a large rock several hundred yards back from the river. He was joined almost immediately by Nathan, and presently Reuben Atwood and Collum Mc-Nicol arrived at the same spot. The two latter knew all about Captain Stanbury's papers, and were to assist in getting them. The little party had previously arranged to meet here secretly for this purpose, and they hoped to complete their task and push some miles down the Susquehanna that same night.

"All here, are ye?" said Collum McNicol, who was the last to arrive. "Let's make haste and have done with the business. My heart is sore after what I've seen yonder this afternoon—"

" Peace, man," interrupted Barnabas. " The less said the better. We're all sore at heart, I'm thinking—aye, an' something more. I feel myself like a panther stripped of her cubs. Don't put fire to our passions, or we'll be tempted to some desperate deed."

" It ain't likely, with not a fire-arm among us," said Atwood. " There's no chance of a shot at Tory or redskin. We must bide our time for vengeance till we're back with the army."

"Aye, we'll have a reckoning then," replied Barnabas. " Every Redcoat will stand for Wyoming—Hist ! who comes ?"

Soft footsteps were heard, and a settler named Morgan Proud glided up to the rock. " Four of ye ?" he said, peering at the group. " I won't be intrudin', men, but I followed hither for a purpose. Do you want arms ?"

" Do we ?" exclaimed Barnabas. "An' kin you pervide them, man ?"

" That I can," said Proud. " When we come up to the fort from Wilkesbarre yesterday—ten of us—we brought nearly two muskets apiece

12

along. But we hid the guns and ammunition down by the river, half expectin' the fort would be surrendered and all arms given up. And we acted wisely—"

"Lead the way, man," broke in Barnabas. " This deed'll win you a golden crown some day. But are you sure the stuff is there yet?"

"They're well hid," replied Proud, "and I told our men, who just started, to take a musket apiece and leave the rest. Will your party join us, Barnabas? We're going down river in flat-boats from Wilkesbarre."

"We have an errand over yonder first," said Barnabas, jerking his thumb northward. "We might ketch up with you, but don't wait on us."

"No, we'll take no risk," Proud answered, "seein' as we'll have women and children depending' on us. But you're welcome to the arms all the same."

Without further speech he led the party obliquely toward the river, and they came speedily to a windfall under the bluff. Proud's friends had been here and gone, but the extra muskets were safe in their hiding place. The man handed out the requisite number, adding a generous supply of powder and ball.

"I'll wait here a bit," he said. "There'll be others coming by, and I have three guns left."

Barnabas and his companions wished him farewell and good luck, and then mounted the bank and struck into the woods. Now that they were armed they felt like new men, and a great weight was lifted from their minds. In single file they made a detour to the rear of the fort, and pressed rapidly northeast through the woods for a mile and a half, speaking not a word on the way. Every heart beat faster as the northern edge of the battlefield was skirted, and now a sharp turn was made to the left. Ten minutes later, as the moon peeped above the horizon, the party reached a little cabin in a clearing. The tears came into Nathan's eyes as he saw the home where his happy boyhood had been spent—the spot sacred to the memory of his lost father. Here was the spring, and there the out-shed where the winter's supply of logs was always stored. The path leading to the step could still be traced between the weeds and grass.

"Cheer up, lad," said Barnabas, divining his thoughts. "It'll all come right in the future. And now we'll be making that search."

They entered the cabin, the door of which was wide open. It had escaped the torch of the Indians, and the interior was much as it had been left on the day when Captain Stanbury started for the war. The end window was closed, but the shutter was off the one in front. The ladder still led to the sleeping-loft overhead, and in the room down-stairs were a table and a broken chair. A few earthen dishes stood on the shelf, and a layer of ashes covered the fireplace.

"It's a bit out of the way," remarked Barnabas, looking around, "an' that's why no one has lived here since. Where shall we begin, lad? Which, to your mind, is the most likely spot? The captain said the papers were under the floor."

"I never knew the boards to be loose," Nathan answered, in a husky voice. "Suppose we try the fireplace."

"A good idea," approved Barnabas. By the light of the moon he scraped the ashes off the big slab of stone that was set in the floor of the chimney, and he was about to pry the stone itself loose when something seemed to occur to him. He straightened up, and glanced toward the door.

"What is the matter?" asked Nathan.

"I'm thinking of Simon Glass," Barnabas answered.

"Why, I forgot all about him," exclaimed Nathan. "He and what was left of his party must have turned back. I didn't see them at the fort."

"But I did, lad," declared Barnabas. "Glass marched in with the Rangers, and that young Godfrey was close behind him."

"Yes, I seen 'em both," corroborated Atwood.

"I was watching the Indians all the time, and Colonel Butler," said Nathan. "So Glass has arrived then? But you don't think he'll give us any more trouble?"

Barnabas only shook his head.

"McNicol," he said, "stand yonder by the door, an' keep your ears to the wood. Watchin' won't come amiss."

The man went to his post, and Barnabas stooped down and lifted the slab. He dropped to his knees, dug rapidly into the dirt with a knife, and lifted out a flat tin box, much rusted. He forced the lid open and handed Nathan a packet of papers sealed with green wax.

The lad pressed it reverently to his lips. "I won't look at them," he declared. "The seal shall remain unbroken until I find my father, or until I am satisfied that he is dead."

"It would be wise to learn the contents, lad," said Barnabas.

Nathan shook his head. "My father's secret is sacred to me," he replied. "If he is alive, he would wish me to guard it, I know. But the papers must not be lost. Will you keep them for me?"

BARNABAS HANDED NATHAN A PACKET OF PAPERS

Barnabas readily—even eagerly—assented. The packet was not large, and he thrust it deep down into one of his wide-topped boots. "It's just damp enough not to crackle," he said, as he dropped the slab back into place, and cunningly strewed the ashes over it again—a wiser bit of forethought than he knew.

"Now," he added. "We'll be off—"

"Hist, men!" McNicol interrupted, in a whisper. "Come hither, quick!"

The three joined the Scotchman at the door, but they did not need to ask what he meant. The forest was alive with whispering voices— with the passage of feet over dry twigs and rustling grass. A light danced among the thick foliage.

It was too late for retreat, and, as the little band crouched behind the shadowy doorway, they beheld a startling sight.

By twos and threes a group of Tories and Indians glided into the glade, close to the spring. The two foremost held a shrinking man between them, and as they came nearer, one said aloud,

in a familiar voice that made Nathan shudder:
" Is this the place, you rebel dog ?"

" It's Captain Stanbury's cabin," muttered the prisoner, who had evidently been made to serve as an unwilling guide.

" You know what you'll get if you're lying," Simon Glass—for it was he—replied with an oath. " Come, men," he added.

" God help us !" whispered Barnabas. "There's no escape unless we kin keep hid. But they're comin' to the cabin, an' Colonel Butler's promise won't count with such fiends. They'll kill every man of us in cold blood."

Low as the words were spoken, they reached the ears of the enemy, and a creaking noise made by McCollum's heavy boots completed the betrayal. " There are rebels here !" roared Simon Glass. " Don't let a blasted one escape ! Surround the cabin !"

" It's all up," cried Barnabas. " Give 'em a volley, an' remember the massacre. Now— fire !"

Four muskets flashed and roared, and, as the

echo fled down the valley, the night rang with yells of rage and agony.

There was no time to look for the result of the volley through the drifting smoke. Barnabas instantly slammed the door shut, and dragged the heavy table against it. "Down, all of you," he shouted. "Stick to the floor. Nathan, you guard the rear wall, an' watch through the cracks of the logs. McNicol, you an' Atwood take the two ends. I'll tend to the open winder here in front."

The three crawled to their posts of duty, and for a time the silence outside was broken only by an occasional moan of pain. The wary enemy had taken to cover at once, until they could learn the strength of their assailants.

"Did you kill Glass?" McNichol whispered across the room.

"He ain't in sight," replied Barnabas. "He moved his head just as I fired. The Tory with him is lyin' dead here on the grass, an' the prisoner is beside him—he's better off, for he'd a been tomahawked anyway. An' there's a wounded Indian dragging hisself past the spring. I won't waste powder on the wretch."

"Glass must have learned where we were bound, and followed us here for revenge," said Nathan.

"It's either that or a deeper motive," Barnabas answered, and even as he spoke a hot fire was opened on the cabin from three sides. The fusillade lasted for several minutes, the bullets tearing through the crevices or burying themselves in the thick logs, but by crouching flat all escaped harm.

As the fire slackened the enemy boldly showed themselves here and there in the moonlight, but they learned a lesson in prudence when McNicol shot two of their number from a loophole, and Atwood picked off a third. Barnabas kept blazing away at the gleam of a torch some distance off in the wood, where a part of the enemy was probably assembled. As nearly as could be judged, the besieging force numbered nearly a score.

"It's a bad lookout," said Atwood, "we can't count on help from any of the settlers."

"More likely the shooting will bring the whole party from the fort," replied Barnabas. "We might make a dash by the rear if there was a winder. The enemy ain't showed up on that side yet."

"They're here now," whispered Nathan. "I see the bushes moving—" Bang! the lad's musket cracked, and with a screech an Indian fell dead. Two more who had been reconnoitering the rear of the cabin bounded into the woods.

"That's the way to do it," said Barnabas. "Load quickly, men, an' don't all let your muskets get empty at once."

An interval of silence followed, lasting perhaps ten minutes, and then a harsh voice from the forest called for a truce.

"Only one kin come near," shouted Barnabas. "What do you want, Glass, if that's you?"

"I'm willing to make fair terms," replied the Tory, who was careful to keep hidden. "Come out and give up your arms, and not one of you shall be hurt.”

“ We’d sooner surrender to a rattlesnake than to you, Simon,” Barnabas answered. “ We’re goin’ to hold the cabin, an’ that’s our last word.”

Glass accepted the ultimatum with a torrent of profanity and threats, and a moment later the firing recommenced. For some minutes the bullets rained against the logs, while the besieged, flattened on the floor, kept watch at loopholes and crevices for any of the enemy who might expose themselves. The plucky little band well realized that their fight was desperate and well-nigh hopeless, but not a word or sign of fear betrayed what they felt.

Presently the firing ceased, and now there were indications that the foe intended to make a combined rush. So certain of this was Barnabas that he summoned Nathan and his companions to the front wall. But for at least once in his life the old woodsman was outmatched. The Indians and Tories advanced only to the edge of the clearing, whence they let drive a straggling volley, and while this diversion was going on, three torches were thrown from the rear upon the roof of the cabin.

A strong breeze happened to be blowing, and with amazing rapidity the flames took hold and spread. The roof was soon burned through in patches, and now the loft floor caught fire. Clouds of suffocating smoke rolled to the lower room, and a shower of sparks and blazing embers made the situation unbearable.

"It's all up with us here," cried Barnabas, " an' there's nothin' left to do but die fightin'. Come, men, let's open the door, give the devils a volley, an' make a rush. Each one for hisself arter that, an' mebbe one or two of us kin reach the woods."

CHAPTER XI

WITHOUT waiting for an answer, Barnabas jerked the table away and swung the door partly open. The enemy were on the watch and immediately opened a hot fire. Two bullets struck Reuben Atwood, and he fell dead across the threshold. The others dodged back into the heat and smoke, and just at the critical moment the firing ceased in response to a loud command.

"It's the Tory colonel hisself," exclaimed Barnabas, as he peeped through a crevice. "He's just arrived, an' there's lots of Royal Greens along with him."

"Colonel Butler," he added loudly, "we'll surrender, providin' you spare our lives."

"Come out first, and then we'll talk," the officer shouted back after a brief pause.

There was hope in the words, and Barnabas

190

and his companions lost no time in scrambling
to their feet.   Half-choked, and sweating from
every pore, they stepped over Atwood's dead
body and staggered across the clearing.   At
sight of the three figures there was a loud murmur of astonishment.

"Where's the rest?" demanded Simon Glass,
as he roughly stripped the prisoners of their
muskets.

"We're all here but one," Barnabas answered,
pointing to the doorway, "an' he's dead."

"I'll send you to join him," snarled Glass,
and with that he presented a gun to the old
man's head.   But before he could fire, Colonel
Butler knocked the weapon aside.

"You ruffian!" he exclaimed.   "Would you
shoot a prisoner in cold blood?"

"He deserves it," remonstrated Glass, in an
injured tone.   "Why, this is the leader of the
rebel band that attacked my party a couple of
days ago, killed four of us, and stole our horses."

"I have nothing to do with that affair,"
snapped Colonel Butler.   "When I want you

to play executioner I'll tell you. Don't interfere again!"

With a scowl Glass slunk away, and for a few moments the officer scrutinized his three captives in silence. The upper part of the cabin was now wrapped in flames, and the red glare made the scene as light as day. Tories and Indians stood grouped in a half-circle, the former with cold, pitiless faces, while the latter looked ferociously at the prisoners under their painted cheeks as they gripped their blood-stained tomahawks and edged nearer with fiendish anticipation. Godfrey, who had been with the attacking party, was standing to the rear, and his face alone expressed pity. He blushed as Nathan discovered him and gave him a quick glance of contempt and defiance.

"You can't expect mercy," Colonel Butler finally said. "Within a few hours after the surrender you are found here with arms in your possession—a direct violation of my terms. And you took the offensive, firing deliberately on a part of my force."

“That’s right, Colonel,” chimed in Glass. “They shot first. We’ve six dead here.”

“We were compelled to fire, sir,” said Barnabas. “We had no way to retreat, an’ that ruffian yonder told his men not to let one of us escape.”

“Exactly,” assented Glass. “But my object was to take you prisoners. I saw you and your men recover the arms you had hidden in the woods, and I was justified in following to discover your purpose.”

At this Godfrey started to come forward, but changed his mind and stopped. His face was pale and haggard.

“Man, you lie,” cried McNicol, turning to the one-eyed Tory. “You never saw us get the guns, and you didn’t even know we were here till you reached the cabin. And had we surrendered at the first, every one of us would have been massacred in cold blood. I know you well, you dirty traitor.”

“Colonel, don’t believe that rebel,” retorted Glass, with a glance of fury at McNicol. “The affair happened just as I said.”

13

"Hang the affair!" testily exclaimed the officer. He moved aside for a moment to converse in a whisper with Captain Caldwell, of the Royal Greens, and then turned to the prisoners. "My duty is very simple," he said. "There is but one question at stake. You were found bearing arms in violation of my terms. You have brought your fate on yourselves, and now—"

"Sir, would our lives have been safe anywhere in this valley without fire-arms?" interrupted Barnabas.

Colonel Butler bit his lip with rage. "You rebel dog," he cried, "do you dare to assert that I can't enforce my own commands? But enough. Captain Caldwell, a platoon of your men, please. Stand the prisoners out and shoot them."

Nathan turned pale. Barnabas and McNicol heard the sentence without moving a muscle. A file of the Royal Greens stepped forward, bringing their musket butts to earth with a dull clatter. But just as several Tories laid hold of the victims to place them in position, an unexpected interference came from Godfrey Spencer.

"Colonel Butler," he exclaimed, "let me speak to you before this goes any further."

"Stop, you fool," muttered Glass, trying to push the lad back.

"Let me go," Godfrey whispered fiercely. "If you don't, I'll tell all."

"What do you want to say?" asked Colonel Butler. "Oh, it's you, Lieutenant Spencer!"

"Sir, I beg you to spare these men," pleaded Godfrey. "With justice to yourself, you can waive the question of their bearing arms, since their object in coming to the cabin to-night was in no wise contrary to the terms of the surrender. We came for the same purpose, and the meeting was accidental. Simon Glass has lied deliberately, and I can vouch for it that he would have shot the prisoners at once, had they given themselves up."

Glass ground his teeth with rage, and had looks been able to kill, the lad must have fallen dead.

"I can't understand this hurried march of your little detachment from the Jersies to Wyoming," replied Colonel Butler. "You told me you were sent by Major Langdon, and now I infer that this cabin was connected with your mission; also, that the prisoners marched from the Jersies with the same purpose in view. I would like a further explanation."

"That I can't give, sir," Godfrey answered firmly.

"Perhaps you can?" and the Colonel turned to Barnabas.

The old man shook his head. "It's a private matter, sir," he replied, "an' my lips are sealed. But what this young lieutenant says is all true."

Colonel Butler looked puzzled and vexed. "Whom did Major Langdon put in command of the party?" he sharply inquired of Godfrey.

"Simon Glass, sir."

"And why were you—an officer of rank— sent along as a subordinate?"

"I don't know, sir. I don't even know fully the object of the expedition."

"Glass, you can explain this mystery," exclaimed the Colonel, losing patience.

"Sir, would you have me betray my trust?" demanded Glass, with well-feigned indignation. "You saw my papers yesterday. You know that they are signed by Major Langdon, and that I am acting under his orders."

"And under mine as well, sir," replied the Colonel, with a frown. "There can be no independent commands while I have control here. Come, we'll drop the question of Major Langdon's authority. I want you to do some work for me to-morrow. You are just the man for it, and you can have the force you led out of the fort when my back was turned."

" I am at your service, sir," Glass replied in a mollified tone.

The Colonel nodded. "You may as well camp here for the balance of the night, and start early in the morning. Scour the whole upper part of the valley, and burn every cabin and house to its foundations."

A wicked smile showed how well pleased the

ruffian was with his orders. "How about the prisoners, sir?" he asked carelessly.

"The sentence stands," Colonel Butler replied grimly. "I will give them a few hours to prepare for death. Hang or shoot them at daybreak."

"I can't entertain your appeal," he added, to Godfrey. "Your arguments do not mitigate the fact that these rebels were found in arms. I must do my duty."

In spite of Glass's angry and threatening looks Godfrey made a second attempt to save the prisoners, but Colonel Butler cut him short in a manner that forbade further appeal. The officer was in an ugly mood, for his natural curiosity to solve the mystery connected with the cabin had been baffled. But matters of more importance demanded his immediate presence at the fort, and without delay he marched off at the head of the Royal Greens.

Glass's first act after the departure of Colonel Butler was to search Nathan thoroughly from head to foot, and the lad submitted with an air of surprise that was more feigned than real; by this time he had an inkling of what it all meant.

The ruffian could hardly conceal his disappointment when he failed to find what he wanted. He proceeded to search McNicol and Barnabas —luckily omitting the latter's boots—and then he reviled the prisoners with the most bitter taunts and insults his brutal mind could invent.

Nathan lost his temper and answered back, thereby receiving a cruel blow in the face; but Barnabas and McNicol stoically endured the shower of abuse. None of the three showed any sign of fear, though they knew they were to die in the morning, and their courage might well have won admiration and pity from a more chivalrous foe. But Simon Glass's half-dozen Tory comrades—who numbered among them the survivors of the squadron of dragoons—were as brutal and degraded as himself. The rest of the force were Indians, and mercy or pity could have been better expected from a pack of panthers than from these blood-thirsty Senecas.

The ruffian finally wearied of his pastime

and walked toward the cabin, which was now nearly consumed. After watching the dying blaze for a moment he returned.

"How soon will those ruins be cool?" he asked of one of his companions.

"I should judge in about two or three hours," the man replied.

Glass looked pleased. "We'd better be turning in," he continued, "for we must take an early start in the morning. We'll hang the rebels before we go. Bring them over yonder now."

He led the way to a thicket of low bushes that stood on the near bank of the spring. In the centre of the thicket were three saplings, and to these the prisoners were secured in a sitting position, with their arms fastened behind them and their backs turned to one another. Having seen that the work was done thoroughly, Glass departed.

"You'd better be praying, you rebels," he said, in a sneering tone, "for your necks will stretch at the first light of dawn."

The night was very warm and the Tories and Indians stretched themselves in groups amid the thick grass that carpeted the clearing. A sentry was posted on guard at the thicket, and as he paced to and fro with loaded musket the upper part of his body was visible to the captives. They could see no others of the party for the bushes, but the silence indicated that all were asleep. Godfrey had kept in the background after Colonel Butler's departure, either for the purpose of shunning Glass or to avoid those he had vainly tried to befriend.

There was no hope of escape, and for a while the wretched little group talked in whispers, each nobly endeavoring to cheer and comfort the others.   None had rested much on the previous night, and finally Barnabas and McNicol fell asleep.

Nathan was now alone with his thoughts, and in the face of death his fortitude almost deserted him, and his mind yielded to bitter anguish. He lived the past over again—his boyhood days here in the valley, his years at college in Philadelphia, and then the string of terrible events that had begun with the loss of his father on Monmouth battle-field. But amid the conflicting thoughts that distressed him the memory of Godfrey's strange words was uppermost.

"What can it mean?" the lad asked himself. "Is it possible that Major Langdon sent Simon Glass here to find and steal these papers? He heard my father tell me where they were, but why would he want to get them? It is a deep mystery—one too incredible to be true!"

Vainly the lad puzzled himself, and at last he fell into a restless sleep. A couple of hours later he awoke with a start, realizing at once where he was, and dreading to find that dawn had come. The moon was far down and under a bank of clouds, and the cabin had long ago burnt itself out to the last spark. But, from the direction of the ruins, floated a dull noise and the sound of low voices.

"Barnabas, are you awake?" Nathan whispered.

"Yes, lad," muttered the old man, and as he

spoke McNicol opened his eyes and twisted his cramped body.

Before more could be said the bushes rustled, and a dusky figure shouldering a musket crept softly into the thicket. Godfrey—for it was, indeed, he—put a finger to his lips. "Hush!" he whispered. "I've come to save you. All are sleeping, except Glass and four of the Indians. They're poking about in the ashes of the cabin, and we must get away before they return. I am going with you, for my life is equally in danger."

He stooped down with a knife in one hand, and quickly severed the cords that held the prisoners. "Now come," he added. "Look where you step, and don't even breathe loudly."

Nathan and his friends rose, trembling with joy, and almost doubting the reality of their good fortune. But they knew by what extreme caution safety must be won, and as noiselessly as shadows they trailed their sore and stiffened bodies behind Godfrey to the farther edge of the thicket.

The young officer had thought out his plans beforehand, and with a warning gesture he stepped into the spring at the point where it became a narrow rivulet, and brawled its course swiftly across the lower corner of the clearing. The others followed, and the murmur of the waters drowned what slight noise was unavoidable.

Now came the critical moment. With anxious hearts the fugitives waded slowly down the stream, crouching low beneath the fringe of tall grass that concealed, on both sides, the sleeping forms of Tories and Indians. On and on they went amid unbroken silence, and at last the dense foliage of the wood closed over them like an arch. They had safely passed the limits of the camp. They waded twenty yards further, and then stepped on land.

Godfrey handed his musket to Barnabas. "You know the country," he whispered. "Lead as you think best."

"We'll make a wide detour back of the fort," Barnabas replied, "an' then come around to the river at the lower end of the valley."

On a brisk trot they started toward the north-west, and as they hurried along the forest trails that the old woodsman chose, Godfrey briefly told what all were anxious to know.

"I got awake a bit ago," he said, and "heard Glass instructing four of the worst Indians to tomahawk you people just before daylight. They were to kill me at the same time, and pretend it was done by mistake. That was to be Glass's revenge for what I said to-night. I remained perfectly still, pretending to be asleep, and when Glass and the Indians went over to the cabin, I decided all at once what to do. I told the sentry I had been ordered to relieve him, and he handed over his musket without a word. He was asleep in two minutes, and my way was clear."

Barnabas and McNicol warmly thanked the lad, and Nathan impulsively clasped his hand.

"I hope we are friends again, Godfrey," he said. "I will never forget what you did to-night."

"I will do more, if I ever get the chance,"

Godfrey answered. "But I can't explain now —wait until we are certain of freedom."

By this time the fugitives were a mile from the enemy's camp, and before they had gone twenty yards further a faint outcry behind them told them that their escape was discovered. All now depended on speed, for it was certain that the Indians, by the aid of torches, would follow the trail with the unerring keenness of blood-hounds.

Barnabas led the little party at a steady pace, taking them several miles to the rear of the fort before he turned parallel with the river. Now they headed for the lower end of the val-ley, and for nearly three hours, while they traversed the lonely and gloomy forest, they heard no sound but the chirp of night-birds and the distant cries of prowling wild animals.

"I can't keep this up much longer," panted Nathan. "The Indians may be close behind, but for my part I believe they've lost the trail."

"Mebbe so, lad," replied Barnabas, "though the quietness ain't an indication of it. We're all badly winded, but the river ain't far off now. Onct we git across, or find a boat—"

The rest of the sentence was drowned by one blood-curdling whoop that rang with awful shrillness through the silent wood. Another and another followed, and the glimmer of a torch was seen coming over a knoll at a furlong's space behind the fugitives.

"The Senecas are hot on the trail!" cried Barnabas, "an' their keen ears have heard us. On for the river! It's our last chance!"

CHAPTER XII

IN WHICH A MYSTERIOUS ISLAND PLAYS A PART

BARNABAS was right in guessing the river to
be near, and the fugitives could not have approached it at a better time or place, though
they had little idea of the good fortune in store
for them. If they thought about the chances
at all, as they ran desperately before the screeching Indians, it was to realize what little likelihood there was of finding a boat, or of safely
gaining the farther bank by swimming.

But when they had plunged through a slope
of water-birches, and straggled breathlessly
down to the pebbly shore of the Susquehanna, a
welcome sight at once met their eyes. Almost
directly opposite, and twenty yards out in the
stream, a big flat-boat was drifting leisurely with
the current.

Over the high gunwales rose two or three

208

heads, and a voice demanded sharply: "Who's yonder?"

"Friends!" cried Barnabas. "Fugitives from the enemy! The redskins are hot upon us. Cover the bank with your guns while we come aboard."

Splash! went Barnabas into the water, and his companions after him. With sturdy strokes they swam diagonally down-stream, caught the stern of the flat, and hauled themselves on board. As they dropped low on the bottom, yells and musket-shots split the air, and bullets rained like hail against the thick timbers.

From the shelter of the elevated bulwark the occupants of the flat returned a cool and effective fire, and when Nathan ventured to peep through a loop-hole he saw two Indians prostrate on the beach and a third struggling in agony in shallow water.

During the lull that followed the first volley from both sides, the boat drifted over a course of rapids, and the swifter current swung it well toward mid-stream. With a few parting shots

14

the baffled foes disappeared, and a peaceful calm fell on river and wood.

The escaped prisoners were surprised to find Morgan Proud and Abel Cutbush on board the flat. The latter's wife and child were with him, and another member of the party was a negro named Cato. Mrs. Cutbush was a hardy type of the colonial women of the time, and her six-year-old daughter, Molly, had not even whimpered during the brief fight.

"It's a good thing we happened to be here," said Proud, when he had gleaned their thrilling story from the fugitives, "and it's all owin' to chance, too. I waited a bit after you left, and as no one came along I pushed down to Wilkes-barre. The people had all fled except Cato here, and Cutbush and his family, and they were tryin' to tinker up this old flat—the only boat left. I helped 'em to stop the leaks and rig bulwarks on both sides, and about an hour ago we got started. There's a couple of other parties ahead of us, but we aren't likely to ketch up with 'em. This old craft is heavy, and it draws a heap of water. I'm thinking we'll stick now and then."

"We'll pull through all right," cheerfully replied Barnabas. "Now that them redskins have turned back the danger is about over, for the enemy will have enough plunderin' and burnin' to do right here in the valley to keep 'em busy. How are you off for weapons? We brought just one with us."

"We have two extra muskets," said Cutbush, "and as Cato ain't much on shootin', his'll make up the number your party will want in case of a possible attack. There's food aboard, and as for ammunition—" He pointed to a keg of powder and a quantity of bullets in one corner of the flat.

By this time the boat had drifted between the abrupt mountains that closed the lower end of the Wyoming Valley, and there was a certainty of good current and depth for some miles ahead. All through the night the men of the party took turns at sleeping and at guiding the flat by means of long poles and a rudder. No hostile shot or yell broke the quiet, and at last the morning sun kissed the blue water into ripples and stained the hoary mountain peaks with gold. Danger was behind, and hope and safety in front.

While Mrs. Cutbush prepared the frugal breakfast, aided by Molly and Cato, Barnabas and Nathan found time to sit in the bow of the flat, where they were presently joined by Godfrey. The lad looked haggard and worried.

"I'm ruined," he said, as he sat down beside his companions. "I feel that I've nothing left to live for. Not that I regret what I did last night. Don't think it. But I shall be branded as a deserter—and worse. I can never go back to Major Langdon, and if I am caught I will be shot or hanged as a traitor. I wish I had never been sent on this wretched business."

"Your mission was not legitimate war," replied Nathan. "Explanations will surely right you. But why worry about the matter at all? You are safe, and can share our fortunes. And after the fiendish acts you saw done at Wyoming by a British force—"

"Stop!" Godfrey said, sadly. "I am still true to my cause, Nathan—as much as you are to yours. Let us not discuss that matter. We can at least be friends while we are together."

"How could we be otherwise, after your noble deed?" replied Nathan.

"Then you have no ill-feeling?" asked Godfrey. "I was afraid you blamed me for that night in Philadelphia. It was Major Langdon who found the note, and he made me go along. I have always wished I could explain."

"Well, it's all right now," said Nathan. "And it was all right then," he added to himself, remembering his reckless flight through the town.

"There is something else I want to speak about," continued Godfrey. "Have you got those—those papers safe?"

"Yes, I have them," Nathan exclaimed, eagerly. "Can you explain the mystery about them?"

Godfrey shook his head. "It is a mystery," he replied, "and a deep one. I only know this. The day after the battle of Monmouth, while our army was at Middletown, Major Langdon sent Simon Glass and a squad of dragoons to Wyoming to get those papers. I don't know why I was sent along, and I never knew until last night that the papers were the property of your father. And Glass—who is the worst ruffian I ever knew—has tried his best to get all of your party killed ever since he learned you were bound for the same place. That's why he was so savage with me last night, when I appealed to Colonel Butler to spare your lives."

"I've had an idea of what was going on for some time past," said Barnabas. "I seen a mighty ugly look in Major Langdon's eyes when he stood over Captain Stanbury on the battle-field. That's when he overheard about the papers, but what in the name of creation did he want with them? Could your father have known him before, lad—over in England?"

"I don't know," replied Nathan. "I never

heard him speak of Major Langdon.   In fact, I don't know anything about my father's past. But I believe the secret to this mystery lies over the sea, and I'll tell you why."

He went on to relate the visit of Mr. Noah Waxpenny to the Indian Queen, and how he had asked information concerning both Richard Stanbury and Major Langdon.   This was new to Godfrey and Barnabas, and all three discussed the matter earnestly, but without coming any nearer a solution.

"We've got to have patience, an' wait," said Barnabas.   "That's the only thing to do.   The papers are safe, anyway, an' this fellow from London may clear up the mystery if we run across him.   Or your father may turn up, lad—"

"Perhaps Godfrey knows something about him," exclaimed Nathan.   "Did the British carry off any prisoners after the battle of Monmouth?"

"Not that I know of," replied Godfrey.   "I saw or heard of none; but then I was in front during the retreat."

"My father is alive," declared Nathan. "I am sure of it."

"I hope so," said Godfrey. "Speaking about those papers," he added, "I feel a good bit worried. If Glass gets it into his head that you have them—as he probably will, when he ·has dug over the ruins of the cabin—he is sure to follow you up."

"It's hardly likely," replied Barnabas. "An' then he can't ketch us anyway, pervidin' the currents and depth of water hold good. No, lad, I think we're done with Simon Glass, as far as this expedition is concerned. There, Mrs. Cutbush has got breakfast ready. She's calling us."

Barnabas and the two lads found no further opportunity that day to discuss the mystery of Major Langdon and the papers. It was a day of hard and unremitting toil. There had been a long spell of dry weather, and, as the river gradually widened, its channel became more and more obstructed by grass-bars, shallows, and outcropping ledges. Doubtless the preceding boats had found a ready passage, but the abandoned flat that Proud and Cutbush had tinkered up under the spur of necessity was broad, heavy, and leaky. Cato was constantly kept busy bailing water, and rudder and poles were of little aid to navigation. Every few minutes all of the party except Mrs. Cutbush and Molly were compelled to get out, and by their united strength drag the craft over the shallows.

By ten o'clock that night less than twelve miles had been covered, and the exhausted men could proceed no further. They encamped on a patch of sand and scrub in mid-channel, and took turns at guard mounting until morning. Mrs. Cutbush and her daughter slept in the flat, on a comfortable bed of dried grass, that was protected from the damp·planks by an under-layer of pine boughs.

" We're about thirty miles below Wilkesbarre, now," said Barnabas, as the journey was resumed after breakfast, "an' it's a good twenty miles yet to the main river, where we'll strike deep water an' the shelter of the lower forts. If I thought

the wadin' and haulin' was to last another day
I'd suggest we take to footin' it on shore."

"It would be a wise plan," agreed Godfrey.
"At the speed we've been making, a force of
Tories and Indians could have overhauled us
twice over, and they may do it yet. You don't
know Simon Glass."

"Don't I?" Barnabas interrupted grimly. "I
reckon I do. But honestly, lad, I believe he's
given up the chase. It's best to take precautions though, an' that's why I spoke of walkin'."

"It won't be easy for me," declared Proud,
shaking his head. "I've got a sprained ankle."

"And my little gal, who ain't no light weight,
would have to be carried," added Cutbush.

"I've been down the river twice before," said
Nathan, "and I'm pretty sure that the lower
part of the North Branch is deeper than up
here."

Several others suddenly remembered the same
fact, from past experience, and so it was decided
to stick to the flat. Godfrey alone favored a
land journey, and he could not hide his appre-

hension at the choice. "If they knew Simon Glass as I do," he said to himself, "they wouldn't lose any time in getting below the forts."

However, after three hours' repetition of the previous day's labors, the channel actually did become deeper and less obstructed. In consequence the current was more sluggish, but the flat drifted steadily on for mile after mile, and there was a fair prospect of reaching the main river that evening.

Early in the afternoon a magnificent buck with large antlers burst out of the woods on the south bank, about a quarter of a mile below, plunged precipitately into the water, and swam for the opposite shore.

"Something scared it," said Nathan.

"A bear or a wolf," replied Barnabas.

"Or a man," Godfrey suggested uneasily.

Barnabas did not answer. He thoughtfully watched the animal until it mounted the bank and disappeared, and after that an extra wrinkle or two remained on his furrowed brow. During the afternoon he scanned both shores intently, and furtively examined the muskets to see that all were loaded.

The sun faded in a haze of gold and purple, and the shroud of night fell on lonely mountain and river. There was no moon, and through the blackness the flat gurgled on its watery way. An hour after dark a misty object loomed out of mid-stream. It was an island, and as the upper point drew near, Cutbush gave the rudder a twist that sent the flat into the channel on the left.

"It's the proper course," he explained, "and the one that we boatmen take. T'other side is full of rocks and shallows."

"But there's a bit of rapids below," said Mc-Nicol, "if my ears don't deceive me."

"They're no account," replied Cutbush. "There's a clean passage through toward the shore side."

He swung the boat further to the left, and it glided silently along within fifty yards of the bank, and three times that distance from the island.

"I've got my bearin's exactly now," said Barnabas. "That's what they call Packer's Island acrost from us, an' a mile or so down yonder on the right is the settlement of Northumberland, where the North an' West Branches meet. We'll be on the main river in half an hour."

"I want to stop at all the forts on the way down," said Nathan, "because the soldiers may have had late reports from the army, and can tell me if my father—"

"Look out, sir," Godfrey eagerly interrupted, turning to Cutbush. "We're running straight into a little island. Don't you see it?"

The men were grouped in the stern at the time, and Godfrey's warning cry, coming so suddenly, startled and confused Cutbush. The result was that he sharply twisted the rudder the wrong way, sending the flat farther toward the shore, and in a direction where the depth of the channel was very doubtful.

Cutbush did not discover his mistake until the others called his attention to it. Then he saw what they meant. Close ahead a triangular promontory of rock and timber jutted in a gradual slope some forty yards beyond the normal line of the bank, and thirty feet straight out from its apex lay the island to which Godfrey had reference. The location was an odd one, and it was a decidedly queer-looking island—a long, narrow cluster of bushy pine trees, pointing up and down stream, and thickly fringed at its base with bushes that seemed to grow straight out of the water.

"It's risky to try that passage," said Barnabas, pointing to the thirty-foot channel between island and promontory, whither the flat was now steadily drifting. "We may find shoals there."

"I give the rudder a wrong turn without thinkin'," muttered Cutbush. "But it's not shoals I'm afraid of. If we float down yonder I won't have time to steer for the rift through the falls, and they're only fifty yards below."

As he spoke he tried to rectify his mistake, and the first two sweeps of the rudder veered the nose of the flat away from the bank. The third swung it broadside across stream, and in this position it bore down on the little island, with a slight diagonal trend toward the wider and safer channel on the outer side. But there was hardly time for this movement to take effect, and the danger of striking was so apparent that Cutbush let go of the rudder—which was as good as useless while the flat was turned broadside—and snatched up one of the poles. He drove it in off the stern, leaned after it till he almost stood on his head, and then rose up with both arms wet to the elbow.

"The pole won't touch!" he exclaimed. "There's easy twelve foot of water here."

"Twelve foot of water!" cried Barnabas; "an' that island only ten yards below! It ain't nateral, man!"

"We're going to strike the island," said Nathan. "Try again."

"No, it's all right," interposed Barnabas. "We're movin' slow, an' there ain't any gravel beach as I can see to stick on. The rear end will strike easy, an' then the flat will swing out toward the far channel."

So Cutbush dropped the pole and the boat drifted on broadside with the current, its occupants calmly waiting the moment of collision. As the distance decreased from ten yards to five, Barnabas craned his neck forward, and shaded his eyes to peer over the lower bulwark. " It's queer," he muttered. " I've been here before, an' I don't mind seein' that—"

Just then a startling thing happened. The whole island was seen to lurch visibly to one side, and at the same instant something flashed and glittered amid the fringe of bushes.

"Look !" Godfrey whispered, hoarsely.

"Down for your lives, men !" yelled Barnabas. "It's a trap! Keep low, an' don't let 'em get aboard."

The entire party dropped like a flash, and grabbed their muskets. A terrible instant of silence followed, broken by a howl from Cato and a whimper of fright from Molly, who was lying flat on the bottom in her mother's arms. Then a volley of shots rang out from the fiendishly contrived ambuscade, and more than one ball tore through the thick bulwark.

But happily no one was hurt, and Barnabas, McNicol, and Nathan at once fired through the three loopholes at which they were posted. A yell of agony blended with another fusillade from the unseen foe, and now a quicker current drove the heavy flat broadside against the mysterious little island.

There was a crash of timber meeting timber and a sound of branches smiting the water. Then, with shrill and blood-curdling yells, four painted Indians scrambled over the bulwark and dropped into the boat. At the same instant a little one-eyed man, holding a musket high overhead in one hand, pulled himself aboard at the bow.

CHAPTER XIII

IT is more than likely that the Senecas and their white allies underestimated the strength of the party in the flat, or else the discovery and demolition of their ambuscade drove them to such desperate measures. At all events, they speedily found they had made a mistake, and in the brief and sharp struggle that followed they got scarcely a show.

Of the four Indians who scrambled over the bulwark three cleared the crouching men and landed beyond them, and the fourth fell heavily on top of Barnabas and McNicol. Before he could use his tomahawk he was pounced upon by the Scotchman, and the two began a lively scuffle.

Mrs. Cutbush carried a loaded pistol at her waist, and while she pushed Molly behind her

226

with one hand, with the other the courageous woman drew the weapon and shot one of the three remaining Indians through the head. The second managed to inflict a severe slash with his tomahawk on Cato's arm, and then Barnabas knocked him senseless with the butt of his musket. The third did not wait to be killed, but with a screech, vaulted over the far side of the boat and disappeared, narrowly escaping a shot that Cutbush sent after him.

At that moment the Seneca who was struggling with McNicol broke away, leaving his tomahawk in the other's hand, and, as he bounded for freedom, Morgan Proud jumped in front of him. They grappled, and fell heavily against the bulwark. The wall of timbers gave way under the strain and both splashed into the river.

There was a quick rush to that side to help Proud, but he and the Indian had disappeared utterly.

As the missing man's friends anxiously scanned the water, a Tory belonging to the attacking party scrambled up in the stern of the boat. McNicol instantly saw him and fired, and the man dropped back with a cry.

Meanwhile, during the entire struggle, Simon Glass had been crouching unseen amid the deep shadows at the bow of the flat, from which place of vantage he had more than one opportunity for a certain shot at his enemies. Now, just as McNicol fired at the Tory in the stern, Nathan caught sight of the figure at the opposite end. With his empty musket in his hand the lad ran toward the spot, little dreaming of the man's identity, or that he was affording Glass just the opportunity for which he had been watching and waiting.

The ruffian rose a little higher, leveled his rifle, and fired. But for the second time he missed his victim at close range, the ball whizzing within a fraction of an inch of Nathan's ear. The report drew the attention of the others, and Godfrey discovered and shot at the Tory just as he made a bound to escape. He half jumped, half fell, into the water, and all ran eagerly to the bow of the boat, which was now drifting slowly down to the falls.

"Was that Simon Glass, lad?" exclaimed Barnabas.

"Yes," declared Nathan, "and he very nearly finished me!"

"There he is!" cried Godfrey, as a dark object rose to the surface near the verge of the falls. An instant later it slipped over and vanished, nor could it be seen again. Equally futile was the search for Morgan Proud and the Indian; beyond a doubt they had perished together.

"It's no use," muttered Barnabas. "Poor Proud is gone. But I have my doubts about that Tory ruffian. He's got as many lives as a cat, an' it's possible he's makin' for shore now, out of sight yonder below the falls."

"Where's the rest of the party?" said McNicol. "It ain't possible we cleaned them all up. We'd better be looking." With this he led his companions back to the stern, past the bodies of the two Indians. Mrs. Cutbush was engaged in binding up Cato's wounded arm, and Molly was sobbing hysterically from fright as she clung to her mother's gown.

The whole affair had transpired in such brief time that the cumbrous boat had moved only a short distance. In plain view above was the mysterious little island, now readily seen to be a long, narrow canoe trimmed with bushes and pine boughs. The collision with the flat had upset it, but it still rested stationary on the water, showing that it was anchored.

There was no sound or motion in the near vicinity, but a subdued splashing in the channel between the canoe and the promontory told clearly enough that some survivors of the enemy were swimming to the shore.

"It ain't likely they can do us any more harm," said Barnabas, "for I reckon their guns an' powder are wet. Of all the infernal tricks I've heard of, that was the neatest. They got ahead of us by land, run across that canoe somewhere, an' anchored it yonder, where they knew we'd have to pass within close range."

"And expecting to pour in a volley, while we were exposed above the bulwarks," replied Nathan.

"Exactly, lad," assented Barnabas, "only we didn't give 'em a chance." Turning to Cutbush, he added : "Better take the rudder, man ; we're nearly at the falls."

Just then Mrs. Cutbush, who was in the bow, uttered a cry, and a tongue of fire was seen to leap up from the bed of dry grass in the middle of the boat. Evidently a bit of wadding had lain there smouldering, and now a breeze had fanned it into a blaze.

Godfrey was nearest, but before he could get to the spot the fire reached an open powder-horn that lay in the grass. It blew up with a dull report, and instantly the whole bed was a mass of hissing, roaring flames. And in the very midst of the blaze, where it had been thrown that morning to protect it from the damp floor, lay the cask of powder. All realized at once their terrible danger.

"It's too late to outen the fire," cried Barnabas. "The explosion may come any moment! Jump for your lives!"

Just then the flat swung over the falls, quivered and tossed amid the rocks and waves, and darted on to the deep and sluggish water below.   Barnabas and Cutbush sprang past the flames to the bow, the former taking Molly in his arms, and the latter grabbing his wife.   They and Cato sprang into the river at the same time that McNicol and the two lads jumped from the stern, and as hard as they could the whole party swam out toward mid-channel, scarcely heeding the two shots that were fired at them from the cover of the bank. They safely gained a cluster of rocks with a fringe of gravel at the base, and from behind this shelter they turned to watch the blazing flat as it drifted by at a distance of twenty feet.

They had hardly looked when a terrific explosion came, casting a red glare all around, and seeming to shake the very bottom of the river.   A shower of sparks and splinters fell,

and huge waves rolled in all directions. For a second or two the shattered craft bobbed up and down, still blazing here and there. Then it lurched under and disappeared, and darkness and silence settled on the scene.

The situation of the little party was now disheartening. They were stranded on a rocky bar well out in the channel, dripping wet, and without means of safely getting away. They were almost defenseless in case of an attack, and to attempt to swim to shore would be a desperate and foolhardy proceeding under the circumstances.

But, in the stupor that followed the explosion, the first impression of the castaways—one and all—was a feeling of intense gratitude for the perils they had escaped, and, before they could realize how badly off they still were, a faint shout came floating over the water, and a dark form was seen struggling toward the rocks from a ledge higher up stream and nearer the bank. The swimmer made a gallant fight against the current, and when he finally gained the bar all were surprised and overjoyed to recognize Morgan Proud.

"Given me up, had you?" the plucky fellow exclaimed, as he clasped hands with his friends. "Well, I had a close call. That redskin stuck to me till we went over the falls. Then we parted company, and after I reached yonder rock I didn't spy him again. I was lying over there getting my breath back when the flat took fire and blew up."

"Did you see anything of Simon Glass?" inquired Barnabas.

"He shot by, swimming like a fish," declared Proud, "and I lost sight of him among the ledges and shoals below my rock. I daresay he got safe to shore."

"I'm sure he did," Barnabas muttered grimly. "So that ruffian is still alive, an' there's likely half a dozen more to keep him company. We're in a pretty tight place, comrades. We can't make the far shore without a boat, an' if we try to swim to yonder bank it means certain death. Glass an' what's left of his party are prowlin' about on watch now—you heard them fire twice as we were swimmin' away from the boat.   An' the worst of it is that we're defenseless."

Immediate investigation proved the old woodman to be right.   Nathan and McNicol alone had held on to their muskets when they plunged from the flat, and Mrs. Cutbush had her empty pistol.   But all the weapons were wet and useless, and though several of the party had a supply of ball, the only powder that had survived the explosion was a small quantity in Proud's water-proof horn.

"It's aggravating to think how near we are to the forts and to Northumberland," said Nathan.   "Glass will hardly dare to prowl about the neighborhood long."

"I'm sure he won't leave yet," muttered Godfrey; "that is, if he knows we are here."

"He does, lad," replied Barnabas.   "The light of the burning flat showed us up plainly when we reached the rocks.   The enemy will do one of two things.   The first—which is to come down an' attack us in their canoe up yonder—I consider unlikely. The second is that they'll lie hid in the timber till morning, expectin' we'll believe they've gone then, an' we'll venture over to shore."

"Hurrah!" exclaimed Nathan, who had suddenly conceived a brilliant idea; "I know how to outwit them nicely, Barnabas, provided they don't try the first of those two plans."

"How, lad?"

"Why, the canoe, of course! I can get it by swimming over to the big island, running a quarter of a mile up the shore, and then swimming quietly down and over to the spot."

"But Glass or some of the Indians may be up there now," said McNicol.

"No," replied Nathan, "I'm sure they are all straight across here watching to get a shot. And they won't see me leave if I keep down in the water."

"The lad is right," declared Barnabas. "It's a good plan, but a mighty risky one, since we can't be certain of the whereabouts of the enemy. But I'll go myself."

"I only wish I could," muttered Godfrey, " but I'm a wretchedly poor swimmer."

" No, I'm going," insisted Nathan. " I am long-winded, and ever since I can remember I could swim like a fish."

" Don't risk your young life, my brave boy," pleaded Mrs. Cutbush. " Leave this to some of the older men."

But Nathan refused to yield, and since he was obviously the best fitted for carrying out the undertaking, and the canoe offered the only means of escape for the party from a most perilous situation, a reluctant consent was finally given.

" Take this to cut the canoe loose," said Barnabas, handing the lad a sharp knife. " You'll likely find it anchored by a rope."

Nathan stripped off all but his light trousers, put the hilt of the knife between his teeth, and swam quickly away from the outer edge of the rocks, followed by anxious eyes and heartfelt wishes for his safety.

Packer's Island extended some distance below

the falls, as well as above, and the current drifted Nathan nearly to the lower point before he struck shallow water. He waded the remainder of the distance, and then ran briskly up the bushy and sandy·shore. The night was dark, but he could dimly make out the jutting promontory when he came opposite it. He continued five hundred yards further toward the head of the island, and then softly entered the water for his diagonal swim of rather more than a quarter of a mile.

Only his head peeped over the surface and a slight ripple trailing behind him was all that marked the gentle strokes of his arms and legs. He was soon in mid-channel, from· where he could darkly make out the canoe. He swam to a point ten feet above it, and dropped down with the stealth of a mink. As he drew nearer he saw that the craft lay bottom up, and was held by a tow rope running down into the water from the bow. A couple of half-submerged pine boughs still clung to it.

The lad caught hold of the rope with one

hand, and with the other he took the knife from between his teeth. He was about to slash when a husky screech made his blood run cold, and he looked up to see the painted face of an Indian glaring at him within ten inches.

The redskin had evidently been shot in the first volley from the flat, and had been clinging to the canoe ever since, too badly hurt to cry out or to swim to shore. But the sight of a hated foe revived his strength, and on the very second that he made his presence known he sprang at Nathan and clutched his throat.

Down went both, entangled with the rope, and tearing it loose from the anchorage in their struggles. The lad kept one hand free, and while he held his breath he stabbed repeatedly with the knife. After a few terrible seconds the grip on his neck relaxed, and he shot to the surface.

The Indian did not reappear, and Nathan lost no time in striking for the canoe. He swung it around by the dangling rope, and started to swim with it down-stream. Bang!

went a musket from the promontory, and a bullet whistled overhead. A second shot followed after an interval of half a minute, but now lad and canoe were on the verge of the open passage through the falls. They went plunging down the slope of spray and waves, and three minutes later Nathan skillfully landed his prize on the outer side of the cluster of rocks.

Nathan's safe return was a joyful disappointment, for his friends had given him up when they heard the firing. In a few words the lad told the story of his adventurous swim, and some of the tributes to his bravery made him blush.

"Now let's be off while we've got the chance," cried Barnabas. "I judge, from the shootin', a part of the varmints are still lurkin' above the falls."

So the canoe was turned right-side up, and the fugitives hurriedly embarked. They were a little crowded, but that discomfort they did not mind.

Either the enemy's weapons were empty, or

else they could not see what was taking place for the darkness of the night. At all events, no shots were fired from the bank, and presently a swifter current took the canoe past the distant lights of Northumberland and out into the broad channel of the main river. The two muskets were reversed and used for paddles, and an hour before midnight the fort at Shamokin was safely reached.

Here the weary fugitives were warmly welcomed, and provided with supper and lodging. Barnabas extracted the packet of papers from his boot, and after drying them over a fire he restored them to their hiding-place. Much to Nathan's disappointment, no news had lately been received from the army; but the tidings of the Wyoming massacre had traveled quickly, and great alarm was felt lest the enemy should advance down the Susquehanna to raid the extensive military stores at Carlisle.

Cato was unfit for travel, and Proud and Cutbush, with the latter's family, decided to remain at Shamokin fort for a few days.

16

McNicol also wished to stay, so that he might visit a married sister who lived at the settlement of Northumberland.

So, at dawn the next morning, Barnabas and the two lads said good-bye to their friends, and resumed their journey down the river in the canoe, satisfied that Simon Glass would give them no further trouble. Indeed, they were by no means sure that the ruffian had escaped drowning.

Below the point of junction of the two branches the current of the Susquehanna was very swift, and the little party traveled rapidly. They made brief stops at McKeesport and the Halifax fort, where they found the same ignorance prevailing concerning the seat of war. Just as the sun was setting they came in sight of Fort Hunter, which stood on a jutting bluff half a mile above the beautiful Kittochtinny Gap, where the river flings itself over a barrier of rocks as it leaves the mountains behind.

Barnabas hauled the canoe high and dry under the stockade, and led his companions up the bank and around to the gate. A sentry was on guard, and after a little questioning he passed the party through. As they went across the yard they observed a horse tied to a post ; the animal was saddled and bridled, and showed traces of recent hard riding.

In the middle room of the block-house something of a stirring nature seemed to be taking place. The new arrivals heard voices raised in shrill and angry dispute, and as they entered they saw two soldiers roughly pushing a man toward a door at one side of the room.

The prisoner was strenuously resisting, and clamoring to be set free, and in his struggles he revealed his face to Nathan. With a thrill of excitement the lad recognized the last man he could have expected to find here.

CHAPTER XIV

IN WHICH NATHAN FEIGNS SLUMBER TO SAVE
HIS LIFE

"UNHAND me, you ruffians!" cried the prisoner, as he continued to resist. "I protest against this brutal treatment. I protest against so unjust a sentence. I am not a spy. I am a non-combatant, and entitled to freedom. I was sent to this country on a legal and private matter by my employers, the firm of Sharswood & Feeman—"

Just then one of the soldiers, losing patience, struck the man a blow between the eyes that felled him to the floor. He was too stunned to make any further resistance or appeal, and his captors flung him into the room and slammed the door.

"Lad, that—that ain't the lawyer chap you spoke of?" inquired Barnabas, as he observed Nathan's agitation.

"The very same!" Nathan cried, excitedly "Noah Waxpenny, of London, who came to the Indian Queen that night!"

"The man who wanted information of your father and Major Langdon?" Godfrey asked, incredulously.

"Yes, that's the one," exclaimed Nathan. "I'm sure he can clear up the mystery. I must speak to him right away."

The lad was too excited to know what he was doing, and before his friends could check him he made a rush for the door of the inner room. But the officer in command of the fort— an ill-featured sergeant—gave him a push that sent him reeling back.

"What are you doing here?" he demanded. "And you?" he added, turning to Barnabas and Godfrey, and regarding them with angry suspicion.

Barnabas briefly explained, and the sergeant was somewhat mollified when he learned that the strangers were fugitives from Wyoming.

"It's all right," he grumbled, "but you had

no call to interfere with my duty. Do you know that spy yonder?" The lad here spoke the name he gives himself—Noah Waxpenny.

"Spy?" exclaimed Barnabas.

"Yes, man; I said spy. I've just given him a trial, and to-morrow morning he hangs."

"What proof have you of his guilt?"

"Plenty," declared the sergeant. "Didn't he come riding by here a bit ago on his way up the river? And didn't we find a paper on him with the written name of Major Gerald Langdon, an officer in the British army? There were two other names, but the first one was enough. It's plain as daylight that the man was sent out to spy the frontier forts along here. I've found him guilty, and I'm going to hang him."

"You'll repent it, if you do," said Barnabas, quickly. "You'd better hold the man, an' report on his case. There ain't enough evidence to hang him, an' what's more, you haven't got the authority."

"Man, I have got the authority," thundered Sergeant Murdock, who was a hard-headed and obstinate Scotchman, very set in his ways, and with an exaggerated idea of his powers. "I'm in charge of this fort, and what I say is military law. The spy hangs at daybreak, and I'll report the case afterward—"

"Sir, you surely won't hang this prisoner?" interrupted Nathan. "He is not a spy, and I can prove it. Let me ask you one question. Was Richard Stanbury's name on that paper?"

"Yes," growled the sergeant, in a tone of sudden suspicion.

"Well, Captain Richard Stanbury is my father," said Nathan, "and he is an officer in Washington's army."

"Then you're the lad the spy was bound up the river to look for, according to the yarn he tells," exclaimed the sergeant. "There's something wrong here. I'm thinking I'll have to put you under arrest—aye, and your companions, too."

"Nonsense!" muttered Barnabas. "This foolery has gone far enough. Don't you know me any more, Murdock? Have you forgot

Barnabas Otter, who was a private in your own company right here at Fort Hunter, after Braddock's defeat? Twenty years is a long time, but you ain't changed much—"

"Man, I'm glad to see you," cried the sergeant, his grizzled face breaking into a smile. "Aye, I recognize your features now. And can you vouch for this lad?"

"With my life," declared Barnabas. "An' what's more, I kin vouch that the man in there ain't a spy."

"You'll have to prove it to my satisfaction," said the sergeant, stiffly.

"I can't prove anything," replied Barnabas, "because it's a good bit of a mystery. But the plain facts of the matter, as far as we know, are these: That man in yonder, Noah Waxpenny, was sent over here from England on legal business—sent over to find Richard Stanbury an' also this Major Langdon. Whether there's any connection betwixt the two is not for me to say. But this much is certain; your prisoner ain't a spy. An' you admit yourself that the fellow

was comin' up the river to search for Captain
Stanbury's son here. He must have learned
that the Captain was dead or a prisoner, an'
that the lad had gone to Wyoming—"

"And he expected to meet me among the
returning fugitives," interrupted Nathan. "I'm
sure that's the way of it."

"What does he want with you?" demanded
Sergeant Murdock.

"I can't tell you any more than Barnabas
has told you," replied Nathan. "It's a legal
and private matter—I am certain of that much.
But if you will let me see Noah Waxpenny he
may be able and willing to explain the mystery.
Please let me speak to him at once, won't you,
sir?"

"No, I won't," snapped the sergeant. "I
don't want another rumpus around here. You
haven't proved the man's innocence and the
sentence of death still stands. And then there
was a third name on that paper—"

"Let me see it, Murdock," interrupted Barnabas.

"I've no objection," replied the sergeant, after a brief hesitation. He and Barnabas withdrew privately to one corner of the room, and as the latter examined the paper that was put into his hands he started visibly and his eyes opened wide with astonishment. For some minutes he and the sergeant conversed earnestly in whispered tones, and then they came forward again.

"Lad," said Barnabas, " my old comrade has agreed to let us see the prisoner in the morning. We must have patience till then."

"Aye, you can see him in the morning," corroborated Sergeant Murdock, "but unless the interview clears up the mystery and proves the spy's innocence he hangs before breakfast. I'm a man of my word and you can count on what I say."

Darkness was now coming on rapidly, and while the sergeant went into an adjoining room to fetch a candle Nathan found an opportunity of drawing Barnabas aside.

· "You saw the paper?" he whispered. "Did it contain any clue?"

"None at all, lad."

"And whose was the third name?"

"I'll tell you again," Barnabas answered, evasively. "Have patience till morning, and I'm thinking all will turn out right. Meanwhile let the matter drop and don't speak. Hush! here comes Murdock back."

That was a long evening for Nathan. It taxed his patience sorely to think that he could not see the prisoner until morning—to know that the man locked up in the little guard-room could reveal, among other secrets, why Major Langdon had made such desperate efforts to get the papers that were buried under Captain Stanbury's cabin at Wyoming. Godfrey was almost equally curious, but Barnabas had forbidden both lads to allude to the matter openly, and the circumstances were such that private speech between the three was impossible.

The capture and examination of Mr. Noah Waxpenny had delayed supper, and after the meal was over Sergeant Murdock unbent and became quite friendly. He showed his guests around the interior of the fort, pointing out the strong features of the stockade, and exhibiting with pride the stores of lead and powder, casks of fresh and salt beef, and barrels of flour.

"I've got only a dozen men here," he said, "and that's as big a garrison as the fort has had for ten years past. But I'm expecting reinforcements up from Harris's Ferry any time now, and the settlers are threatening to come in on account of the rumor that Butler's force will be marching down the river from Wyoming."

The rest of the evening was spent on the grassy knoll at one side of the enclosure, where Nathan and Godfrey related their adventures at Wyoming to an interested audience, and Barnabas and the sergeant discussed old times between whiffs of their pipes. At intervals Noah Waxpenny could be heard groaning dismally, or tramping up and down the narrow limits of his cell.

At ten o'clock Sergeant Murdock went his round, posting one sentry inside the stockade gate and another at the rear of the fort, where a small window opened from the guard-room. A third was put on duty in the middle room of the block-house, with instructions to watch the prisoner's door.

From the left of this middle room opened the big room where the privates slept, and on the right were the guard-room and the officers' quarters. To the latter's apartment, which contained a number of straw pallets spread on the floor, the sergeant led his guests. "All fixed, are you?" he said. "Good night, then, comrades." He blew out the candle, turned over, and was soon snoring loudly.

A little later the slow and regular breathing of Godfrey and Barnabas told that they, too, were slumbering. Nathan envied them, for try as he would he could not induce the least symptom of drowsiness. For a long time he lay with wide-open eyes and active brain, thinking of the promised interview in the morning and listening to the occasional footsteps from the adjoining guard-room, where Noah Waxpenny seemed also to be possessed by the demon of wakefulness.

When the lad finally did fall asleep from sheer weariness his rest was disturbed 'by hideous dreams. From one of these he suddenly awoke, relieved to find himself safe in the fort instead of battling with blood-thirsty savages out on the river.

As he listened to the regular breathing of his companions he fancied he heard a low groan from outside, and almost immediately a rustling noise at the open door of the room fell on his ear. Closer and closer came the soft and stealthy sound, and the next instant, to the lad's unspeakable horror, the dark figure of a man kneeling on all fours rose at his very side, and a hand was passed gently over his body.

Nathan's heart almost stopped beating, but by a tremendous effort he choked back the cry that was on his lips. For, at that moment, his eyes being partially accustomed to the gloom, he saw that the man held a glittering knife between his teeth; and he realized that at the first shout for help the blade would be plunged into his breast.

He was terribly frightened, but by exerting all his will power he succeeded in doing what was best under the circumstances. He feigned sleep, and lay perfectly motionless. Not a muscle quivered, though cold sweat started on his face and hands. All he could think about was that glittering knife. It did not occur to him to wonder who the man was, or what he wanted.

The unknown intruder was deceived by the ruse. With both hands he lightly and deliberately pressed every part of the lad's clothing from his throat to his feet. Twice he went over him, and then a whispered curse testified to his disappointment at not finding what he wanted. Next, he took the knife from between his teeth with one hand, and as he lifted it high to strike, he turned a little toward a window in the side wall, dimly revealing a scarred and wrinkled face with but one eye.

Nathan uttered a shrill cry, and grabbed the

descending wrist with both hands. A desperate jerk lifted him upright, and he heard the knife clatter to the floor. He held tight for a second or two, and then a blow on the face broke his grip and hurled him back.

He sprang quickly to his feet, crying out in chorus with his companions, who were now awake and stumbling blindly over the floor. He saw a dark figure, followed by another, rush into the yard. Then the men at the other end of the block-house woke up with noisy clamor, and amid all the din, a musket-shot rang loud and clear.

" What's wrong?" demanded Sergeant Murdock. "Speak, somebody!"

"Simon Glass was here," cried Nathan. " He tried to kill me. He just ran out! Don't let him get away!"

The name of the Tory ruffian was familiar to all, and the angry and excited men swarmed from both sides into the middle-room. A private appeared on the scene with a lighted lantern, and by the yellow glare the door of the guard-room was discovered to be wide open.

"The spy has escaped," roared the sergeant. "This is Glass's doing! I wish I'd hung the man last night!"

"Glass didn't come here for that," declared Barnabas. "Waxpenny must have opened the door an' run fur it when he heard the row in yonder; an' where's the sentry?"

Just then a clamor rose from several of the men who had hastened outside. Led by Sergeant Murdock, the rest of the party ran into the yard, and at one side of the door they found the prostrate body of the sentry who had been posted in the middle-room. The man was breathing faintly, and his swollen and purple face showed that he had been nearly strangled to death by a pair of muscular hands.

With shouts of vengeance the crowd scattered in different directions, but a cry from Barnabas brought them together again at the partly-open gate of the stockade. Here lay the second sentry stone dead, with a long knife buried in his ribs.

17

"If Simon Glass don't die for this may I never shoulder a musket again!" roared the infuriated sergeant. "It was a sharp trick he played. He must have come here a bit ago, persuaded the sentry to admit him, and then stabbed the poor fellow to the heart. Next he enticed the other sentry to the yard, and settled him, too. And after the lad here discovered him in the room both he and the spy darted out the gate."

"But where's the third sentry?" cried Barnabas, "an' who fired that shot—Hark! some one's calling now!"

Indeed, the shouting had been going on at intervals since the first alarm, but owing to the noise and excitement the man had not been able to make himself heard. The sounds came from the rear of the block-house, and thither the whole party ran in haste, to find Private Mickley prancing up and down on one of the lookout platforms.

"Where've you been?" he yelled, hoarsely. "Why didn't you come sooner? I've been keeping watch on the ruffian, but now he's gone—escaped in that big canoe."

"Escaped!" cried Barnabas. "Why didn't you stop him?"

"Man, explain yourself," roared the sergeant. "Quick! find your tongue!"

"Ain't I telling you?" sputtered the angry soldier. "Give me a chance. When I heard the first yell I run round to the front just as a little man dashed out the door. He was making for the gate, but when he seen me he changed his mind and cut for the rear. I fired at him. and missed, and just then out pops the spy. Before I could lift my empty gun he was past me and out the gate. So I let him go, and went for the other. I got round here in time to see him scramble over the stockade. I reckon he didn't know the drop that was below him, for when I looked over the platform he was lying stunned in the bushes down yonder. I kept watching him and singing out for help, and all at once up he gets, staggers like a drunken man to the canoe, and goes a-paddling down stream with all his might. I'm thinking his one leg was broke."

"How long ago was this," thundered the sergeant.

"Not two minutes, sir."

"Then he ain't far off," cried Barnabas. "Have you another boat handy?"

"There's a little canoe in the creek above the bluff, with two paddles in it," replied Sergeant Murdock.

That quickly Barnabas was off, calling to the lads to follow him. Nathan and Godfrey were at his heels as he scaled the stockade at the upper end and plunged down the sloping bank to the creek. They found the canoe at once and jumped in, and a moment later the light craft had swung from the creek's mouth to the river. The lads were paddling, and Barnabas crouched amidships just in front of them.

"Murdock, we're goin' to get the assassin," he shouted.

"Good luck to you!" the sergeant called back. "I wish I was as sure of overhauling the spy."

The canoe was quickly past the fort, gliding like a duck on the swift current, and now the other craft was dimly sighted about a hundred yards down stream.

"I knew he couldn't be far," muttered Barnabas. "Paddle hard, lads. He can't do much with that heavy boat. This is going to be the last of Simon Glass, or else the last of me."

"We have no weapons," exclaimed Nathan.

"Neither has he, lad, or he would a-fired at the sentry who tried to stop him."

"I hope he won't take the shore when he sees we're after him," said Godfrey.

"He's too badly hurt to do that," replied Barnabas. "No; we're goin' to get him. I feel it in my bones. He'll pay with his life for venturin' this far after them papers. When he lay in ambush that night he must have heard us speak of stopping at the forts, an' I reckon he tramped all this distance alone."

During part of the above conversation a bend of the river had concealed the fugitive from view, and now, as the pursuers swung around, the two canoes were seen to be less than forty yards apart. Glass was close to shore, struggling desperately to drive his heavy and unwieldy craft, while with scarcely any effort Nathan and Godfrey urged their lighter boat forward.

The distance rapidly decreased to twenty yards—fifteen—ten. Now the ruffian's scarred face could be seen by the moonlight that was breaking through the clouds, as he looked back at quick intervals. And shortly ahead of him was the line of noisy rapids, white with dashing foam and spray, black with outcropping bowlders and ledges. ·

"We'll hardly ketch him this side the falls," muttered Barnabas. "It ain't an easy passage. Watch sharp for the rocks, an' don't—"

Just then Simon Glass dropped his paddle and twisted himself around in the stern. "I won't be taken alive!" he yelled, "and I'll kill one of you first." With that he drew a big pistol, leveled it at Barnabas, and fired.

CHAPTER XV

JUST at this critical instant, when almost certain death threatened Barnabas, a fortunate thing happened. The bow of the Tory's canoe struck a half-submerged rock, and the sudden jar spoiled his aim, so that the bullet passed a foot above his intended victim.

In the twinkling of an eye the long craft swung around, lodged fore and aft across a narrow passage of the falls, and turned bottom up. Out went Glass, head-first into the foaming waves on the lower side.

There was no time for his pursuers to sheer off, and scarcely an instant later the second canoe crashed into the obstruction and swung broadside against it, though luckily without capsizing. But the shock pitched Barnabas out of the bow, and with a vain attempt to grab the canoe in front he glided off the slippery bottom, and was borne down the stretch of boiling rapids. The lads caught a brief glimpse of him as he bumped into Glass, who had lodged on a spur of rock twenty feet away. Then both were washed off by the furious current, locked together in a desperate struggle, and the gloom hid them from view.

"Barnabas will be drowned!" cried Nathan. "And we can't do anything to save him! We're stuck tight!"

"We've got to get loose!" exclaimed Godfrey, and with his paddle he struck the forward boat a terrific blow. To his delight it grated free at the stern end and whirled around, and that quickly the two canoes were bounding side by side amid the perilous falls, swinging this way and that, leaping high over crested waves, and rebounding from the cruel rap of hidden ledges.

Any attempt at steering was out of the question in so mad a current, but the lads hardly thought of the danger. Before they could realize it, their canoe had dashed safely down the roaring, raging slope, and was cleaving the choppy little waves that marked the even flow of the river beyond the rapids.

With anxious hearts, and with a fear that they dared not put into words, Nathan and Godfrey paddled swiftly along on the current, eagerly watching ahead and out toward midchannel, and over to the near-by wooded shore. The moon was under clouds again, and the surface of the river was misty. Frequently they shouted the name of the missing man, but only the sullen voice of the rapids answered.

When they had gone nearly a mile, some lingering hope persuaded them to turn back. So they pushed up along the shore from eddy to eddy, scanning every patch of sand and gravel, every clump of bushes, and constantly calling Barnabas by name. Hope was utterly dead when they drew near the falls, and now Nathan grounded the canoe in a little cove. Tears were rolling down his cheeks, and he was not ashamed of them. "We've got to face the worst," he said, hoarsely. "Barnabas is drowned. He and Glass perished together."

"Yes, there's no doubt of it," assented Godfrey. "I'm awfully sorry for you."

"If we could only find the body," said Nathan.

"But we can't," Godfrey replied. "The water seems to be deep around here, and they both must have gone to the bottom. They may not come to the top for a day or two."

Nathan groaned. "This is terrible," he exclaimed. "I can hardly believe it. To think that Barnabas is dead—that we will never see him again! You don't know how brave and noble he was—"

"Yes, I learned that much during the last few days," interrupted Godfrey. "Believe me, Nathan, I am as sorry as you are. To know such a man as Barnabas Otter makes me feel sometimes that your cause will triumph."

Nathan silently clasped the other's hand and for some minutes the two lads sat without speaking, gazing over the misty waters and listening to the sad music of the falls.   Then both heard a distant and muffled clatter of hoofs.

"Horsemen!" exclaimed Nathan, "and they are coming up the river road.   I must see them."

"But there may be danger," remonstrated Godfrey.

"No, not in this neighborhood.   It is too close to the fort and to Harris's Ferry.   Come on, Godfrey!"

They sprang out of the canoe and clambered up the wooded bank, reaching the road just as two wagons came along, escorted by six mounted men.   Nathan halted the party, and after briefly explaining that he and his companion were fugitives from Wyoming, he told what had happened that night at Fort Hunter.   The victims of the tragedy were known by name to the men, and they expressed genuine sorrow for the death of Barnabas, as well as heartfelt relief at the termination of Simon Glass's infamous career.

"We're bound for Shamokin fort with supplies sent by the commissary-general of Pennsylvania," stated the leader of the party. "I suppose you lads will go along back with us to Hunter's? Just hop into the wagons yonder."

Before either could reply one of the men in the rear dismounted and came forward. With an exclamation of surprise he clapped Nathan on the shoulder.

"Corporal Dubbs!" cried the lad. "How did you get here?"

"Why, you know I was on the sick-list the morning the Wyoming troops left camp," the corporal explained, "and when I got a little better the general sent me to the Board of War with dispatches. Then I learned that my brother was lying up at McKee's fort with a bullet wound he got at Wyoming, and I'm on my way there now to see him."

"And was there any news of my father when you left camp?" Nathan asked impatiently.

"That's what I want to tell you," replied the corporal, drawing the lad aside. "Your father is lying at the house of a loyal farmer named

Welfare. His place is near the head of the Shrewsbury River, and not far from Monmouth. Welfare himself brought word to the camp the day I left. He said the captain was badly hurt, and wouldn't be able to be moved for a month."

Nathan was speechless with joy for a moment. "Then my father is really alive?" he cried. "I was sure of it. And do you think he is still at the farmhouse?"

"I'm pretty certain he is," replied the corporal. "I don't know how he came there, or anything about his injuries, but you may count on it, he is in good hands."

"I'm going straight to him," declared Nathan. "I'll travel day and night."

Corporal Dubbs nodded approvingly. "That's the best thing you can do," he said. "The sight of you, lad, will be better than medicine for the captain. There's a stage from Harris's Ferry to Philadelphia in the morning. You can catch it if you hurry. Don't forget the place, and be sure you ask for Jonas Welfare.

And be careful when you get in the neighborhood of the Shrewsbury, for the enemy are
making raids over that way from New York."

"I'll remember," assented Nathan. "I must
go now. We have a canoe below, and I mean
to catch that stage. Will you tell Sergeant
Murdock at Fort Hunter that Barnabas is dead
and ask him to find the body and—and—bury
it—"

The lad's voice broke, and for a moment he
could not speak.

"In Barnabas's left boot," he added, "is a
packet of papers that he was taking care of for
me. They belong to my father. Will you
ask the sergeant to keep them until they are
sent for?"

Corporal Dubbs readily promised, and with a
hearty clasp of the lad's hand he mounted and
rode after the now moving wagon-train.

Nathan and Godfrey hurried back to the
canoe and were soon paddling swiftly down the
river. The roar of the falls faded behind them,
and when a curve hid the fatal spot from view,

Nathan turned with tear-dimmed eyes for a last look.

"You forgot about Noah Waxpenny," said Godfrey, when the lads had paddled some distance in silence.

"So I did!" exclaimed Nathan. "I hope Sergeant Murdock won't catch him, and if he does I don't believe he will dare to hang him. As for that mystery—why, I'll get my father to explain it."

"Then you are going straight to see him?"

"Straight," declared Nathan. "You heard what Corporal Dubbs told me. I'm going to travel as fast as I can. And what will you do, Godfrey, I don't want to part—"

"Nor do I," Godfrey said hastily. "At least not yet. If I thought I could safely accompany you—"

"You can," interrupted Nathan. "I'm sure of that. And I want my father to meet you."

Godfrey smiled sadly. "I'll go with you," he replied, "and then I'll watch for a chance to take boat from the Shrewsbury to New York.

I intend to report to Major Langdon, come what may."

"I suppose that's the best thing you can do," assented Nathan, "but I was hoping you might have changed your mind about—"

A look on Godfrey's face made him stop thus abruptly, and for half an hour nothing was said. Then the day began to dawn, and about the time it was fully light the stockade and houses of Harris's Ferry hove in sight around a bend of the river.

CHAPTER XVI

IN WHICH A PEEP AT THE STATE-HOUSE LEADS TO AN UGLY ADVENTURE

HARRIS'S FERRY—now the populous capital city of Harrisburg—was, in 1778, a small and unimportant place. John Harris, an old Indian trader and the founder of the town, lived here. Some years before, he had made the acquaintance of Captain Stanbury, when the latter stopped at the ferry on a trip from Philadelphia to Wyoming. Nathan was aware of this fact, and resolved to make use of it at such a time of need. So, after the lads had landed and given their canoe in charge of an old boatman, they climbed the river bank and presented themselves at the door of John Harris's big stone mansion.

The old trader was at breakfast, early as was the hour, and he gave his visitors a cordial greeting even before he had heard their story. Nathan's explanation gained much sympathy and a ready promise of assistance. There was little time to spare, but the lads tarried long enough to eat a hearty meal. That finished, the trader took them to the bank of the river directly opposite his house, and pointed out the mulberry-tree to which he had been tied by hostile Indians some years before, and where he would have been burnt to death had not aid arrived in the nick of time.

Then, in haste to the Three Stars Tavern on Front Street, where the Philadelphia coach, with three elderly passengers inside, was about ready to start. John Harris paid the fares, and after shaking hands with the lads and bidding them come to see him again, they mounted to the outside seat beside the driver. A couple of minutes later the blasts of the coaching-horn rang through the little settlement, and the long ride had begun.

Nothing worthy of special mention took place during the journey. Passengers got on and off, stoppages were made for fresh horses and meals, and the nights were spent at wayside towns.

The lads' incidental expenses were paid by the driver, in accordance with secret instructions given him by the kind-hearted trader.

Lancaster was reached on the evening of the first day, and here the night was spent. The two following days were rainy, and the muddy condition of the roads made traveling slow. The lads remained outside, sheltered by a sail-cloth hood that was stretched over the top of the seat. Under other circumstances they must have enjoyed the journey, but the shadow of the terrible events they had so lately passed through was still upon them. They could not forget the horrors of Wyoming, the vexatious escape of Noah Waxpenny, and the tragic death of Barnabas Otter and the Tory ruffian. Nor was the future free from worry. Nathan felt a burning impatience to reach the Shrews-bury, and he could not rid himself of the fear that he would find his father either dead or gone. Godfrey, on the other hand, was con-cerned not a little for his own safety. In spite of the assurances of his companion, he believed himself to be in danger. And there was some ground for this fear. The lad, though not a spy, was still a British officer and loyal at heart to the cause of the enemy. And he was on his way to Philadelphia, where there was a strong likelihood of his being recognized as one of that hostile army which had occupied the city during the previous winter.

Nathan tried to inspire his friend with confidence, and partly succeeded. Neither cared to be· questioned concerning their past adventures and their future plans, so they held aloof at all times from their fellow-passengers. The driver was a garrulous fellow, but fortunately with an inclination to do all the talking himself. This just suited the lads, and from morning till night they listened with feigned interest to his accounts of coaching experiences and his remarks on passing scenery.

On the evening of the fourth day after leaving Harris's Ferry, just as dusk was falling, the coach rumbled down to Middle Ferry on the Schuylkill, and the passage across in a big flat-boat was quickly made. Then followed a short ride through the fields and woods in the cool of the evening, and a spirited dash down Chestnut Street, where the good citizens of the town were smoking and gossiping at their front-door steps. Taranta, taranta, tara! sounded the horn as the lumbering stage turned into Fifth Street at the corner of the State-House, and a minute later the panting steeds drew up at their destination—Homly's Inn at Fifth and Walnut Streets. The painted face of Benjamin Franklin beamed a welcome from the creaking sign-board that swung under a lighted lantern, and there was further encouragement to the thirsty and hungry travelers in the following printed couplet:

> "Come view your patriot father! and your friend,
> And toast to freedom, and to slavery's end!"

Nathan and Godfrey climbed down from the high seat, and stood looking about them. Of the half-dozen passengers in the stage some had already entered the inn, and others had trudged away in the shadows of the night.

"The dear old town again!" said Nathan; and a tear glistened in his eye. "It seems too good to be true!"

"I know how you feel," replied Godfrey, "and I'm sorry I can't feel that way myself. But all I'm thinking about is getting away from a place where recognition will mean danger."

"And I'm in as big a hurry to leave as you are," said Nathan. "There are miles and miles between me and that farm-house on the Shrewsbury where my father is lying wounded—perhaps dead."

"Not that," Godfrey answered quickly. "You will find him getting well—I'm sure of it. And where are we going first? Not to the inn, I hope—"

"No," interrupted Nathan, "I'm too anxious to see Cornelius De Vries. We'll go straight there, and get supper and a night's rest, and then we'll arrange about the rest of the journey."

"Lads, there's good cheer to be had inside," called the driver, as he started to lead the horses to the stable-yard. "Homly's the man to give you a meal and a bed."

"Thank you, but we have friends here," Nathan replied.

"All right! Good-bye, and good luck to you!"

"Good-bye!" the lads answered; and then they started briskly up Fifth Street. They reached Chestnut Street, where there were plenty of lights and people, and crossed to the opposite side. On the corner Nathan halted and turned around.

"There's no danger," he said, noticing his companion's uneasiness. "We'll go on in half a minute—I want to take a look at the State-House. There's a light in the big hall, and up yonder hangs the dear old bell—the bell that rang out liberty for us two years ago."

"For you, not for me," Godfrey gently reminded.

"Oh! I forgot!" Nathan exclaimed contritely. "Forgive me, old fellow. I should have known better than to stop you here—we'll go on now."

But it was too late. During that brief interval of delay, unobserved by the lads, a ragged and sinister-looking man of middle age had been staring keenly at Godfrey, whose features were partly exposed to the glimmer of a street lamp. Now he came quickly to the spot, barring the way up Fifth Street for the lads.

"It's you, is it?" he said insolently, with a leer of malice at Godfrey. "I thought I weren't mistaken. And what are you doing in Philadelphia, my fine British officer? Did you just wake up and find the red-coats gone? Or did you come over from New York to look about a little—"

"You are mistaken, my good fellow," interrupted Godfrey, his face turning slightly pale.

"Get out of the way," Nathan added angrily. "Don't stop us here—"

"I'm not mistaken," the man asserted loudly; "not a bit of it. I know who I'm talking to—your name's Spencer, and you were here with the British last winter. Don't be in a hurry to get away, you and your friend."

"Who is he—do you know him?" Nathan asked in an undertone.

"I do now," Godfrey whispered. "His name is Burd, and he kept a store up near the barracks. I had him arrested by the guard for threatening Major Langdon. He's going to give us trouble, Nathan. Look, the people are beginning to notice us—"

"Whispering treason, that's what you are," exclaimed the ruffian. "No such doings, my fine fellows. It's lucky I saw you—"

"We must get away at once," muttered Nathan. "What a fool I was to stop you here! Now will you get out of the way?" he added to the man. "You're making a mistake that will cost you dear—I am a son of Captain Stanbury of the American army, and a soldier myself—"

"A likely story!" sneered the ruffian; and that quickly, as the lads started to move, he threw himself upon Godfrey and bore him hard back against the corner of the house. "A spy! a spy!" he yelled at the top of his voice.

Nathan lost his temper completely, and like

a flash he fetched the man a stunning blow in the face that made him release Godfrey. A second blow sent him staggering to the edge of the sidewalk, where he set up a prodigious shouting for help.

Clamor and confusion followed, and escape for the lads was out of the question. As they stood side by side against the wall they were quickly hemmed in by an excited mob, and so deafening was the noise that they could not make themselves heard. Men came running from every direction—citizens, store-keepers, tavern loungers, lads eager for a fight, and a few crippled and bandaged soldiers.

"Spies! spies!" they howled. "Kill them! hang them!"

Nathan, feeling himself to blame for the trouble, stepped a little in front of Godfrey. He had a pistol in his pocket, and this he pulled out with a flourish, though he hoped to avoid the necessity of using it.

"Listen, my good people!" he shouted. "There must be some here who know me. I

NATHAN PRESENTED HIS PISTOL

am an American soldier, and my companion is
not a spy—"

It was no use. He could not make himself
heard. Closer and closer pressed the mob, in-
flamed and urged on by the ruffian, Burd.
The sight of the lad's drawn pistol kept the
foremost back a few paces, but those in the rear
began to hurl missiles. Stones and clubs struck
the wall on both sides of Nathan, and a rotten
apple burst on Godfrey's shoulder. The crowd
was increasing, and the clamor was waking
noisy echoes in other quarters of the town.

Nathan's pallor gave way to a flush of anger.
"Keep back!" he roared. "Keep back, or I'll
fire. You cowards! Give me a chance to
speak."

The uproar deepened, but the circle widened
a little at the ominous look of the weapon.
Then, just as a rush began in the rear, a hoarse
shout of "The watch! the watch!" rose above
the clamor of voices. The sound of dull blows
were heard, and right and left through the parting crowd, wielding their staves at every step,

came a dozen men of the town watch. At their head, and seemingly acting as the leader, was a man wearing a sword and a military coat. Without ceremony he snatched Nathan's pistol.

"Keep close to me," he commanded, "and walk boldly."

At once the men of the watch surrounded the two lads and led them quickly across Chestnut Street. The crowd followed, hooting and yelling, but taking good care not to venture within reach of the staves. Right into the State-House marched the officer, the watch, and the prisoners, and a moment later Godfrey and Nathan crossed the threshold of the large chamber on the eastern side of the first floor—the same in which the memorable Declaration of Independence had been signed.

Here several lights were burning, and a number of men were standing about in groups. The watch had halted in the hall, but the officer entered with the lads, and turned to a man who had just come forward. The latter was tall and wore a long cloak of light material. As the glow of a lamp flashed on his face it revealed the familiar features of General Washington.

"Sir, I have obeyed your orders," said the officer. "These young gentlemen were the cause of the disturbance, and they can explain for themselves. I think you will recognize one of them—"

"Nathan Stanbury!" exclaimed Washington. He held out his hand, and the stern expression of his face relaxed.

"It is I, sir," replied Nathan, stammering in his surprise. Before he could say more two arms were thrown around him from behind, a kiss was planted on his forehead, and the familiar voice of Cornelius De Vries cried: "My dear lad! God be praised!"

Again and again the worthy old Hollander embraced the lad, giving him scarcely a chance to breathe. Finally, in his delight, he turned to Godfrey, and would have embraced him as well. But Washington held up his hand with a smile.

" Master Stanbury," he said, " I did not expect to find you in Philadelphia so soon, nor was I certain that you had escaped the bloodshed at Wyoming. It affords me the highest pleasure to know that you are safe, for I assure you that I have not forgotten your valuable and trusty services in the past. But a short time ago I was telling Master De Vries how gallantly you fought at Monmouth, and what a narrow escape you had from hanging when you saved my papers at Valley Forge."

" You do me too much honor, sir," said Nathan, with a blush.

" Not enough, my brave lad," replied Washington. " But come, I forget that you may speedily fall in my good graces," he added, in a jesting tone, " since you are accused of disturbing the peace of this good and loyal town of Philadelphia. You shall give me an explanation, and account for your companion."

" That I will gladly do, sir," declared Nathan.

" But I can spare you only a little time," added Washington. " I left my army at White

Plains, on the Hudson, and made a quick journey here to confer with some of my Quaker friends on matters of importance. I must be starting back by morning, and before my presence becomes generally known in the town. And I prefer to talk apart from these worthy gentlemen."

He led the way to a far corner of the room, bidding Cornelius De Vries follow himself and the lads. With as much brevity as possible Nathan told his story, and he was careful to omit nothing, since he knew that the whole truth would be best for the interests of Godfrey.

Washington listened intently, now smiling, now frowning at parts of the narrative. "I have already heard the news from Wyoming," he said, when the lad had finished, "but not so clear an account as yours. You seem to have displayed your usual bravery and clear-headedness, Master Stanbury, and you have certainly had more than your share of perils and adventures. I deplore the loss of Barnabas Otter,

who was a trusty and valuable man, and I regret that you have not fathomed this strange
mystery with which your father seems to be
connected. I confess that it has a deep interest
for me. As for the recent brawl out in the
street—why, it seems that you are not to blame.
But it was imprudent for your companion to
have entered Philadelphia, and I hardly know
what disposition to make of him." He paused
a moment, smiling. "Is he disposed to turn
patriot?"

"He is not, sir, with all due respect to you,"
Godfrey answered, firmly.

"Let him accompany me, sir," exclaimed
Nathan. "He risked his life to save myself
and my friends. He is not a spy, and he
should not be held as a prisoner. Help him to
get back to the British lines."

Washington shook his head. "I can't do
that," he replied. "I can't lend my aid to
such a purpose. But Master Spencer deserves
to be rewarded for his gallant conduct, which I
do commend most heartily. So I shall let him

accompany you to visit your father, Master Stanbury, and I dare say he will be making a little trip over to Long Island one of these days. Is that satisfactory?"

"Quite so," replied Godfrey, with a smile, "and thank you, sir."

Washington turned to Nathan. "Now, my boy, you will want to get speedily to your father?" he asked.

"As soon as possible, sir," Nathan replied, eagerly. "Please tell me how he is? Have you heard lately?"

"At last accounts he was doing well, but he was not able to be moved, else I should have sent a party for him. I will not deny that he is in some danger of capture by raiding-parties of the enemy, so you had better get to him without delay. What is your opinion, Master De Vries?"

"I agree with you, sir," answered the Hollander, "much as I should like the lad to spend a day or two with me in Philadelphia. But it is all for the best."

19

"Yes, I must start at once," assented Nathan. "And how shall we go, sir? By land?"

"I think not," replied Washington; "the roads through the Jersies are bad and lonely, and you would run a risk of meeting bodies of the enemy. As it happens, there is a sailing vessel lying now down at South Street wharf, and I can arrange with the captain to take you along the coast and up the Shrewsbury. He and his crew are loyal and trusty men, and have been engaged in secret service for me for some time past. Master De Vries," he added, "you know the place and the man. Suppose you make the necessary arrangements at once, and as soon as that is done the lads can go secretly to the river. By then the streets will be quiet."

"It is a wise plan, sir," agreed the Hollander, "and I will see to the proper arrangements."

He departed immediately, and then Washington drew Nathan a little apart from Godfrey.

"I can spare but a moment more," he said,

in a low tone. "You are a brave lad, Master Stanbury, and an honor to your country and to your father. I shall not forget you in the future, and I predict that you will have an officer's commission before you are much older. I will speak to you of other matters at a better opportunity. I trust that you will reach your father safely, and that he and you will speedily be within the shelter of my lines at White Plains. When you leave the farm-house with him come by way of New Brunswick, where you will find American out-posts. You will both be needed. A battle cannot be long delayed, and by this time the French fleet has probably arrived off Sandy Hook. As for Master Spencer, to whom you owe much—why, I leave his interests in your hands, and I trust no harm will befall him."

Washington shook hands with both lads, and spoke a word of farewell. Then he joined the gentlemen who were waiting for him, and an aid shortly conducted Nathan and Godfrey to another apartment of the State-House. Here they remained three hours, at the end of which time Cornelius De Vries returned to announce his complete success. The town was now quiet, and the lads safely reached South Street wharf. It was not quite midnight when they parted from the old Hollander and went on board the sloop "Speedswift," and when they came on deck in the morning, after a good night's rest, the vessel was many miles down the Delaware.

No British men-of-war were met with, but, owing to bad weather, the voyage was prolonged to nearly a week—a delay that sorely tried Nathan's patience.

At last, one dark and sultry July night, the "Speedswift" entered the mouth of the Shrewsbury, and sailed cautiously along the south shore.

When the channel became shallow a small boat was lowered, and two of the crew rowed the lads to a point near the head of the river. The captain, who knew the locality thoroughly, went along with the party, and when they lauded in a little cove he pointed to a road that skirted the north shore of the river.

"That's your way, my young gentlemen," he said. "Follow the road for two miles, and you'll come to Jonas Welfare's place. You can't miss it, for it's the first house."

A moment later the boat was pulling back to the vessel, and the two lads were walking rapidly toward their destination. Nathan was in a state of doubt and suspense—now confident of finding his father, now fearing that he was dead or captured. He kept Godfrey almost on a run, and after half an hour's tramp they reached an old stone farm-house standing in a yard full of pine trees.

No light was to be seen, and with a fast-beating heart Nathan mounted the porch and rapped on the door. It was opened almost immediately by an elderly man, who carried a candle in his hand.

He looked at the lads suspiciously, and with an air of disappointment, and then gruffly demanded their business.

"Are you Jonas Welfare?" Nathan asked, eagerly.

"That's my name, sir."

"Well, I am Captain Stanbury's son. Is— is he still here?"

"Captain Stanbury's son?" exclaimed the farmer, incredulously. "Yes, you look like him. Come right in."

The lads followed Mr. Welfare into the hall, and after closing and barring the door he led the way to an apartment on the left. Here a lamp was burning, and in a large chair sat a bearded man with sunken eyes and pale and hollow cheeks. With an eager cry he rose to his feet, and the next instant Nathan was clasped in his father's arms.

Godfrey discreetly stepped back into the hall, and when he entered the room five minutes later, the farmer had left it by a rear door. Nathan was kneeling by his father's side, and the captain's hand rested lovingly on the lad's head.

"Who is this?" he asked, looking up. "Did he come with you, my boy?"

"He is an old friend," replied Nathan, motioning Godfrey to sit down. "He saved my life. But I will explain presently. You have been very ill, father. Are you getting better and stronger now? Tell me all about it."

"I have improved wonderfully in the last week," replied Captain Stanbury, "though it will be some time before I am quite myself again. And there is but little to tell, my boy."

His face suddenly became grave, and he fixed his eyes on the floor.

"The wound I received at Monmouth was more painful than dangerous, and when I came to my senses I was a prisoner with the enemy's rear-guard of Hessians. After carrying me some miles on the retreat they brutally assaulted me with bayonets and clubbed muskets, and left me for dead along the road. This kind-hearted farmer found me and brought me here, and to him and his faithful wife I owe my recovery."

"I was sure you were alive," said Nathan. "I never quite lost hope, father, and now you will want to hear my story—"

"Yes, if you can make it brief. There are reasons, my boy. I heard of your perilous journey through Jonas Welfare, and when news of the Wyoming massacre reached me I feared greatly for your safety. God has been very good to us both."

"I will tell you all about the journey," said Nathan, "but there is something to come first." In a few words he related Noah Waxpenny's visit to the Indian Queen tavern, and mentioned the name of the legal firm that he represented. "The man was trying to find you, father," he added, "and also Major Langdon, of the British army."

Captain Stanbury's face turned even whiter, and there was a strange look in his eyes. "Sharswood & Feeman, Lincoln's Inn!" he muttered, half to himself. "It has come at last, after all these years! And at a time when I despise and spurn it for myself! But for the sake of my son—" He paused abruptly. "You should have told me this before, my boy," he added.

"I had so little chance," Nathan replied, "and most of the time I forgot it."

"And have you seen this man since?"

"That is part of my story, father. I am coming to it—"

"Go on quickly, lad. I am listening."

Accordingly, as briefly and clearly as he could, Nathan described his adventurous travels, telling how desperately Simon Glass tried to get the papers for Major Langdon, and how Godfrey saved the lives of the prisoners. He told all the leading incidents of the cruise down the river, and concluded with the escape of Noah Waxpenny from Fort Hunter and the sad death of Barnabas.

Captain Stanbury listened with a countenance as rigid as marble, and when the story was done he rose to his feet and feebly paced the floor half a dozen times. On his agitated features were depicted grief, passion, and unutterable horror. Finally he paused in front of the lads, and took Godfrey's hand in his own cold and trembling grasp. "My brave boy, I want to thank you," he said hoarsely. "Your conduct has been indeed noble. I could not feel more gratitude and respect for you were you a patriot at heart, instead of one who has clung to the cause of oppression. But party feeling shall make no breach between us. Sir, you are a hero."

Turning to Nathan he went on hastily, and with an air of confusion: "This is a terrible story, my boy, terrible. I hardly know what to make of it. By God's mercy you have escaped death a dozen times over. And so Barnabas Otter · is dead! You say he perished with this Tory ruffian. A braver man, and a truer friend never lived. But the packet of papers, my boy? I fear they are lost."

"They will be recovered with the body," replied Nathan, "and if Noah Waxpenny has not been caught—"

"Never mind about him," interrupted Captain Stanbury. "The papers are the most important, and for your sake I trust they will be found."

"For my sake!" exclaimed Nathan. "Father, what does this mean? Why do you speak and act so strangely? What did Major Langdon want with the papers, and why is Noah Waxpenny seeking you both?"

Captain Stanbury pressed one hand to his brow, and a look of anguish appeared on his face. "My boy, you shall know all," he said, in a tone of hoarse resolve. "Sooner or later the truth would have to come out. Major Langdon is—"

Just then the rear door opened noisily and Jonas Welfare hurried into the room. "Captain, they are coming!" he exclaimed. "I hear the tramp of the horses on the road."

CHAPTER XVII

"Coming, are they?" said Captain Stanbury.
"Well, I am ready." He buttoned his coat
across his breast, and picked up a hat that lay
on the table. "Can you furnish a couple of
extra mounts, Welfare?" he added.

"Yes, I can fix you," said the farmer. "I
have three horses in the barn."

"Father, where are you going?" exclaimed
Nathan.

"I am about to leave this noble gentleman's
house for a safer refuge," Captain Stanbury answered. "To be brief, my boy, I fear I am in
some danger. Last night the farmer's hireling,
a surly fellow, whom I have long suspected, vanished mysteriously. I concluded that he had
gone to New York to denounce me, and Welfare
shared my opinion. He spent the day in beat-

300

ing up a score of loyal yeomen, and they are now here to take me to New Brunswick. You and Godfrey will go along, of course. The fact that the enemy have been raiding almost nightly between here and Sandy Hook, made a large escort necessary for my safety."

Meanwhile the muffled sounds of hoofs and a jangle of equipments had been heard in the yard, and, now, just as the Captain finished his explanation, there was a sharp rap on the front door.

"Is that you, Ruggles?" the farmer called loudly, as he led his companions into the hall.

"Yes," was the almost inaudible response. "Open quickly!"

"It's a strange voice!" gasped Welfare. "We are betrayed—the enemy are here!"

"Already," murmured the Captain. "It can't be possible!" Godfrey and Nathan turned pale.

There was a brief wait, and then the rap was repeated. "Open in the King's name, Jonas Welfare," demanded an angry voice.

"Who are you? What do you want?" cried the farmer.

"We want the rebel officer whom you are sheltering," came the reply. "If you value your life you will let us in at once. The house is surrounded, and it is useless to resist."

Welfare snatched two loaded muskets from a rack on the wall, and gave one to the Captain. "The first red-coat that tries to break into this house, dies," he shouted loudly.

"My good sir, this won't do," Captain Stanbury said firmly. "You shall not risk your life for mine. Open the door and let them take me."

"Never," declared the farmer. "I'll protect you as long as I can. Man, do you want to end your days on one of those rotten prison ships?"

"I am likely to die more speedily," muttered the Captain, half aloud, and a terrible expression crossed his face. "You had better open the door, Welfare," he added, "but first find a hiding-place for these lads. Their presence can hardly be known, and this one will probably be hanged if he is found here."

"I know that, sir," interrupted Godfrey, "but I will stand by the rest of you."

"And so will I, father," Nathan cried, hoarsely. "Do you think I would desert you at such a time? Mr. Welfare, can't you give me a gun or a—"

Crash! A musket butt thundered against the panels of the door. Crash! crash! The blows rained hard and fast, and the timbers began to split. The farmer cocked his weapon, and held it ready.

"I'll keep my word," he muttered. "If we can hold out a bit the yeomen may arrive—"

"By that time the house will be taken," cried Captain Stanbury. "There is only one course, Welfare." He stepped toward the door, but before he could reach it the report of a musket rang loudly, and a clatter of hoofs was heard on the road. Then came yells and cheers, the pounding ceased, and there was a rush of heavy feet off the porch. Crack! crack! crack!

Firearms were blazing noisily, and the night rang to the din of angry voices and frightened and plunging steeds.

"Our fellows have arrived," cried the farmer, "and are engaging the enemy."

"God grant they conquer!" said Captain Stanbury, throwing an arm around Nathan's shoulder.

For two or three minutes the fusillade and din lasted. Then a bugle note rang clear, followed by triumphant shouts and furious clatter of hoofs.

"The enemy are off!" cried Welfare. "We are saved!"

As he spoke the porch echoed to the tread of many feet, and hearty voices demanded admission.

The farmer flung open the shattered door, and half a dozen sturdy yeomen pushed into the hall, bearing in their arms a motionless form clad in a red coat.

"We just got here in time, Jonas," cried the leader of the party. "The enemy are kitin' for Sandy Hook, with two-thirds of our boys at their heels. We shot three of 'em, but we lost poor Lige Garret. And here's a British officer with a bullet in his breast."

"Put him on the couch in the room yonder, Ruggles," said the farmer.

The wounded man was borne in and laid down, and a pillow was pressed under his head. Nathan and Godfrey, who had drawn near out of curiosity, were startled to recognize Major Langdon.

"It's all up with him," said Ruggles. "I know the signs. A little brandy might make him last longer, though it's a doubtful mercy."

"I'll get some," replied Welfare, hurrying to a closet and producing an earthen jug. A drink of the potent liquor had a speedy and reviving effect on the Major. He lifted his head a little, and opened his glassy eyes. There was blood on the breast of his coat, and a few drops oozed from his lips.

Just then Captain Stanbury came forward, and at sight of the wounded officer he uttered a low cry.

20

"My good fellows, I wish to speak to this man alone," he said, hoarsely. "Be assured that I have a sound reason. Pray leave us together for a few minutes. Nathan, you remain. And you, too, Godfrey."

All the rest left the room, wondering at the Captain's agitation and request. Welfare, who went last, softly closed the door after him.

For a moment Major Langdon stared silently at Captain Stanbury and the lads, and it was evident that he knew all three. His face was white with pain, but it showed no trace of anger or hatred. In his eyes was a look of unutterable self-reproach and contrition.

"Dick," he whispered faintly, "this is the end."

"Yes, I fear it is," said Captain Stanbury. "God have mercy on you! Nathan," he added, "this man is my younger brother Gerald—my brother and your uncle!"

"Your brother!" gasped Nathan, and Godfrey uttered a cry of astonishment.

"It is a strange story," resumed the Captain.

"Let me tell it in a few words. My father was the Earl of Ravenswood, and at Ravenswood Court, near Nottingham, in England, the three brothers of us were brought up. Anthony, the eldest, died in 1760, and that same year I married the daughter of a retired sea-captain of Bristol. Mary Harding was the equal of any woman in the world, but my father chose to think that I had disgraced him and the family. We had a bitter quarrel, and he disowned me and cast me out. Being the oldest living son, I was then Lord Langdon, but I cared nothing for the title. I came to Philadelphia under an assumed name, Nathan, and there you were born and my beloved wife died. Since then I have lived only for you, my boy, and that you might some day come into your inheritance, I preserved the papers relating to my marriage and your birth. They were in the packet you found under the floor of my cabin. And from the day I left England I neither saw nor heard of my brother Gerald until we met after the battle of Monmouth."

Captain Stanbury sank into a chair, covering his face with his hands, and for a moment there was deep silence. Nathan neither moved nor spoke. It was a strange story he had just heard. So Major Langdon was his father's brother—his own uncle! The mystery was growing clear, and he shrank from what he suspected was to come.

Godfrey seemed also to understand, for there was a look of fixed horror on his face.

"Dick," said Major Langdon, "it's my turn now. I can't last long, and I want to confess—"

"No, no," interrupted Captain Stanbury. "Let that rest, Gerald. It can do no good to tell it."

"But I must," persisted the dying man, in a shrill voice. "Do you think I can go to my grave with such a burden on my soul? I came here to-night to kill you, Dick, and I have been justly punished. God knows I am repentant—"

"I believe you are, Gerald."

"Thank you, Dick. Now let me speak while I can—let me tell it all. I recognized my nephew in Philadelphia, and you I discovered on the field of Monmouth. I heard you speak of the papers, and it was then I first conceived this awful crime. I wanted the title and estates —I wanted to be Earl of Ravenswood, Dick, and you and your son stood in the way. But I hated you both because you were rebels, else I could hardly have gone so far. I had you carried off the field, and I told the Hessians to kill you—"

"I suspected that, Gerald. I saw and recognized you when you rode by me to the rear. But I was too weak to speak."

"And do you know what I did next, Dick? Do you know that I sent a band of ruffians to steal the papers—that I paid Simon Glass to kill your boy—my own nephew?"

"Yes, I know that, too. I heard it from Nathan, who was mercifully saved from death."

"And can you forgive me, Dick? I have no

right to ask it, but I am truly repentant.   You won't refuse a dying man?"

Captain Stanbury leaned over and took his brother's hand.

"Gerald, I do forgive you," he said. "I have no right to be a judge, and you are paying the last penalty of your sins."

A look that was almost peaceful came into Major Langdon's eyes. He gasped for breath, and feebly raised his head higher.

"I shall die happier now," he said, "as happy as any man in my circumstances can. But what are you doing here, Spencer? I can't understand it."

In a few words Godfrey explained, and the Major smiled faintly. "You did right, my lad," he whispered. "I am glad that Glass is dead, and that he failed in his purpose. What a wretch I have been! I sent you along, Spencer, so that Glass would know my nephew from his resemblance to you. It is a strange likeness, and I have often wondered at it."

He was silent for a moment, struggling with

pain and weakness. When Godfrey poured some brandy between his teeth his face flushed and he gained fresh strength.

"Dick," he whispered, turning to his brother, "you will go home now, won't you? I received a brief letter a month ago informing me of father's death. So you are the Earl of Ravenswood, and your son is Lord Langdon."

"I want neither the title nor the estates," exclaimed Captain Stanbury, almost fiercely. "I am a true American, Gerald, and after what I have seen of this bitter war I wish no more to do with England. And yet, for my son's sake—"

"I, too, am a true American, father," interrupted Nathan, his eyes flashing with excitement. "Do you think I would go and live in England?—that I would take title or fortune from King George, our bitterest foe? Never, father, never! My blood boils when I think of Wyoming! Let us stay here and fight for our rights, like true patriots. I am glad those papers are lost, and I hope they will never be found."

"Nobly said, my boy!" cried Captain Stanbury, in a voice that shook with emotion. "I would not have had you choose otherwise—"

At that instant a commotion arose outside—loud voices mingled with the neighing and clatter of horses. The front door opened, and a strangely familiar sound brought the hot blood to Nathan's cheeks. Then footsteps crossed the hall, and into the room strode Barnabas Otter.

The scene that followed can be better imagined than told. With a grin of pleasure Barnabas shook hands with his friends, thereby convincing them that he was not a ghost. Nathan was half-laughing, half-crying, as he embraced the old man, and looked almost incredulously into his rugged face. Major Langdon watched the scene curiously; his glazing eyes and leaden hue told that the end was very near.

"It's me, sure enough," cried Barnabas, when the first greetings were over. "Here's your papers, Captain," producing the packet from his boot. Captain Stanbury shrugged his shoulders as he took them, and Nathan did not try to hide his disappointment.

"So they aren't any account after all, lad," said Barnabas, in a sympathetic tone. "It's hard luck! You see I've been made acquainted with the whole story."

"What do you mean?" asked Nathan.

"You'll know soon," Barnabas replied. "Wait till I tell you how I escaped death—it's not a long yarn. You may remember that the Carson House stands on the Susquehanna half a mile below the Kittochtinny Falls. It seems that after Braddock's defeat the family dug a secret passage from the cellar of the house to the river, so's they might escape by water in case of an Indian attack. Well, Glass an' I were sucked under the bushes into the secret mouth of that passage. We were both unconscious at the time, an' when I come to after a bit I didn't know where I was. I hollered three or four times, an' down come Carson an' his son with lanterns. Simon Glass was stone dead, an' I reckon they buried him the next day. I pushed right up to Fort Hunter, learned from Corporal Dubbs where you lads were gone, an' then struck for Harris's Ferry. There I run across Noah Waxpenny—"

"So the sergeant didn't catch him?" interrupted Nathan.

"No, lad. We came on together to Philadelphia, and then across the Jersies here. Waxpenny is out yonder now, washin' off the dust of travel. He's a queer chap, but—"

Just then Mr. Waxpenny himself entered the room, looking as fresh and clean as though he had just stepped off ship.

"I am informed that Major Gerald Langdon is here," he said, rubbing his lean fingers. "Also Captain Richard Stanbury and his son. I have the honor to represent the firm of Sharswood & Feeman, solicitors, Lincoln's Inn, London. They sent me to this country in the interests of their late estimable client, the Earl of Ravenswood—"

"Your errand is already known," the Major interrupted, faintly. "My minutes are numbered, and what you have to tell no longer concerns me. But there stands the new Earl of Ravenswood, and his son, Lord Langdon."

"Sir, these gentlemen have no claim to the titles," said Mr. Waxpenny.

"No claim?" demanded the Major. Nathan and his father looked surprised, and Barnabas nodded at them meaningly.

"I said no claim," repeated Mr. Waxpenny. "The Earl had—a third and elder son, Anthony—"

"He died years ago," gasped Major Langdon.

"Exactly, sir; but he left a wife and son behind him."

Having made this announcement Mr. Waxpenny paused a moment to enjoy its thrilling effect. "Anthony Langdon was a wild and dissipated young man," he continued. "Under an assumed name he was married in London in the year 1759. In the following year, after a son had been born to him, he tired of his family, deserted them, and came home. A week later he was stabbed in a drunken brawl in Nottingham. Before he died he confessed his marriage to his father, who chose, for reasons that may be understood, to keep the secret locked in his own bosom."

Mr. Waxpenny stopped to stroke his chin. " The deserted wife," he resumed, " was a proud and high-spirited woman. Feeling satisfied that her husband had tired of her, she emigrated to America with her father and her son, where the Earl kept track of them for a time. They were worthy and upright people, and the knowledge of this fact doubtless prompted him to make confession and restitution on his death-bed. By the terms of his will, which was entrusted to my employers, one-half of the estate is divided equally between his sons Gerald and Richard. The other half goes to Anthony's son, who is the rightful Earl of Ravenswood."

" Have you found him ?" asked the major.

" I regret to say that I have made no progress as yet," replied Mr. Waxpenny. " The lad would now be eighteen years of age. The name of his maternal grandfather was Matthew Marsham, and he himself was called by the assumed name of his father, Godfrey Spencer—"

Godfrey sprang forward, his face as pale as ashes. "Sir, my grandfather was Matthew Marsham," he cried. "I am Godfrey Spencer, and my mother is still living."

Mr. Waxpenny tried hard to preserve his legal dignity, but the effort was vain. "You are Godfrey Spencer?" he exclaimed excitedly. "Yes, you have the family likeness. And can you prove your claim?"

"My mother has the papers, sir—the certificate of her marriage and my birth."

"Then you are the Earl of Ravenswood," declared Mr. Waxpenny, rubbing his hands with delight. "My Lord, I congratulate you." He made the lad a sweeping and impressive bow.

Godfrey blushed with confusion, and looked around him in a dazed manner. "It seems like a dream," he said. "I can hardly realize it. Major Langdon is my uncle, and so are you, Captain Stanbury—"

"And you and I are cousins, Godfrey," cried

Nathan. " I am glad to hear of your good fortune, and I don't envy you one bit. I wish you all happiness and prosperity."

" Thank you, Nathan," Godfrey replied huskily, and the lads affectionately clasped hands.

*　　*　　*　　*　　*

It is now time to drop the curtain. After several hours of unconsciousness, Major Langdon died peacefully at daybreak, and was buried a few hours later in a grove of oaks near the farmer's house. As soon as the sad ceremony was over the whole party started for New Brunswick, under the escort of the yoemen.

From there Godfrey and Noah Waxpenny pushed on to New York. The lad was sick of the war, and a week later he sailed, with his mother and the law-clerk, for England, where he speedily proved his claim to the title and estate of the deceased Earl of Ravenswood.

Captain Stanbury, Nathan, and Barnabas rejoined Washington's army, and fought bravely until the surrender of Lord Cornwallis at

Yorktown ended the long struggle, and gave the United Colonies their freedom.

A few months later Godfrey persuaded his uncle to accept half of the late earl's estate, and with a portion of the money, Captain Richard Langdon—to give him his rightful name— bought a handsome property in the suburbs of Philadelphia. There he and Nathan lived happily together, keeping up their old friendship with Cornelius De Vries, and occasionally visited by Barnabas Otter, who had gone back to his beloved Wyoming Valley at the close of the war.

In after years, when his father was at rest on the banks of the Delaware, Nathan made more than one visit to his ancestral home in England, where he and Godfrey lived over again in the past, and the ties of kinship that connected the cousins were not more strong than the memory of the distant days when they had suffered and fought together for the sake of Captain Stanbury's mysterious papers.

THE END

www.ingramcontent.com/pod-product-compliance
Lightning Source LLC
Chambersburg PA
CBHW031152120726
47905CB00006B/1924